This novel is e

The names, cha

are the work of

CW01669034

Any resemblance or act relating to any

persons, living or dead, locations or

events involving them, is entirely alleged

or coincidental.

Proof read/editing by Zeldos
Cover art by Orphan Press, Leominster

NATIONAL TREASURE
Ben Nevis and the Gold Digger Book 2

CHAPTER 1

Harry Cohen had said she was a '*national treasure*'. That's what he'd said on the phone: 'Wear a decent suit, she's a *national treasure.*'

She didn't look much like any type of *treasure* to me, let alone a *national* one – buried treasure maybe; found, dug up, and needing bit of restoration.

Harry had called me on the office phone that morning.

'I've got a job for you, Ben, not the usual type. Can you come round later?'

'*Not the usual type*' sounded interesting. The usual type of job for Harry Cohen, 'Theatrical Agent to the Stars' – well, that's what his business card says, although most of the stars he handles are burnt out and on their last twinkling. The majority of his clients these days are young Z-list celebrities nobody has heard of who do a couple of reality television series where the blokes flex their abs and the girls get their tits out and then they disappear – the usual job I do for Harry is security: keeping people at a fair distance from one of these Z-listers when they open a supermarket or similar major cultural event in their brief time in the public eye, or keeping screaming girls away from Harry's latest boy band and getting them from the concert venue to their hotel and keeping them there. Are you getting the vibe that I'm not impressed by these 'stars'? You're dead right, I'm not. So a '*national treasure*' had sounded intriguing. The lady in his office wasn't.

Harry Cohen's offices took up the first floor of an updated Victorian building in Wardour Street, very handy for the theatre area of London and for the offices of a host of other agents and entertainment production companies. Being in central London there's no parking of course, so rather than pay the exorbitant NCP charges I took a leisurely stroll across London Bridge from my office in the Borough High Street and wound my way through the tangle of streets to his lair. I like doing that in London, taking in the vibes and energy of the place. It never sleeps and hardly ever pauses for breath. Love it.

I wore a decent suit like Harry had asked, but kept the faith with my social class with a Status Quo T-shirt. Harry pulled his semi-obese body up from the large swivel chair behind his large desk in his large office, with large pictures of his stable of talent on the walls, as his secretary showed me, in using one hand to push my hand off her shapely backside. It was just a bit of fun; we'd known each other a long time, ever since I started working for Harry about six years ago when he'd been one of my first clients after I left the Met and went solo, and his recommendations to others in the entertainment industry had brought a lot of business my way so I felt I owed him a bit.

He stood and came round to shake my hand. Everything with Harry was large – the office, the swivel chair, his desk, his cigars, his ego, *especially* his ego – and lots of things with Harry were also a bit far from the truth, like the large pictures of Tom Hanks, George Clooney, Robert De Niro and Joe Pesci on the wall, with Harry's agency details overlaid in the corner. No doubt those major stars do have UK representation, but it ain't Harry Cohen; not unless they're up for *Love Island* and *I'm a Celebrity Get Me Out of Here*.

The '*national treasure*' was sitting this side of the desk facing Harry, so I couldn't get a good look as I entered.

'Ben, thank you for coming,' Harry said as he pumped my hand. 'I don't think you've met Marcia before, have you?' He waved a hand towards Marcia, who I took to be the '*treasure*'. She stood and turned towards us. 'Ben Nevis, Marcia Johnson. Marcia Johnson, Ben Nevis.' Harry beamed his introductions. The name didn't register with me. One thing that did was that she didn't remark on my name; most people who meet me for the first time do. I guessed Harry had filled her in on the fact that I had been named after a Grand National winner that my dad had won a bundle on, and not a bloody mountain. Good. We won't have to go through that old story again.

We shook hands, she retook her seat, and Harry fetched a chair from the side of the room for me and put it down in front of the desk where we could all see each other. Bells were ringing in my head; I sort of recognised this lady. She was in her early sixties, slim and elegant in a tailored brown trouser suit, dark ankle boots and bluish-gray shirt that matched her hair, which was in a multidimensional pixie cut. Impressed on my fashion knowledge, eh? Google. But what struck me most about Marcia Johnson were her eyes. Cornflower blue, striking – could be colour contact lenses, but nevertheless striking. So, as I said before, '*treasure*'? The face looked haggard and was the part that needed restoration: lined, bags under her eyes, and a grey tinge to the skin. A worried face, very worried; sort of lady my mum used to call '*mutton dressed as lamb*'.

'You want a coffee, Ben?' Harry asked.

'No, I'm fine thanks.' I've lost count of the number of times I've asked Harry to get a proper coffee machine, but the tight bugger still has his secretary use the rubbish from jars.

He spoke to Marcia. 'As I told you earlier, Marcia, Ben has worked for me on a variety of occasions over the last ten years, and if anybody can find Janie he will.'

Ah, now I was getting the story. Who was Janie? Wayward daughter run off with boyfriend the family don't approve of? Or maybe she was a much-loved dog that had been stolen?

'Tell Ben what you told me.' Harry sat back and puffed on one of his large cigars.

Marcia Johnson gave me a weak smile and a resigned look of worry, together with a small shrug of her shoulders, 'Well, Mr Nevis, I really can't tell you an awful lot. Janie is my daughter; twenty-two and a sensible girl, a serious actress, stage and screen.' She paused as Harry stood and leant across the desk to pass me a 10x8 standard colour promo pic of Janie. She was a stunner; sharp chiselled features under a balayage lob haircut – Google again – a slim body in sensible blouse and skirt and a wide smile. Marcia Johnson carried on. 'I haven't heard from her for a fortnight, nothing. Her phone is dead and her flat is empty. It's so unlike her, Mr Nevis, we talk every day, we shop together. She wouldn't just go off without telling me, she just wouldn't. I'm so worried.'

She was welling up. I can't stand it when females cry. Harry stepped in offering a tissue across the desk.

'Can you find her, Ben?' He raised his eyebrows at me. 'She opens at The National in a month – she's missed rehearsals which she would never normally do. Something's wrong, as Marcia said. This just isn't like her at all.'

I put on my sympathetic face. 'I can have a go. You could register her as a missing person?'

'Should I?' Marcia Johnson looked from me to Harry.

Harry waved the suggestion away. 'I'd hold on a couple more days, give Ben a chance to have a look for her first.'

I liked his confidence in me. Or maybe it was his worry at the press getting the story and the National cancelling her contract, and with it his commission – probably the latter.

'Married? Divorced? Any boy friends?' I asked, the usual '*your starter for ten*' questions.

Marcia Johnson shook her head. 'No, not married or divorced. As for boyfriends, I don't know – none that she ever spoke seriously about.'

Looking at Janie Johnson's picture I was bloody sure she had boyfriends; they'd be queuing up for this lady.

'Close friends? Member of any clubs, or a gym? Car owner?'

'Oh, so many friends – but I've called all those I know, and none have seen her. I think she belongs to a local gym, but I don't know of any other clubs. She has a car but it's still outside her flat. She has a parking space.'

'Okay, well first off I'd like to have a look around her flat.'

Marcia Johnson picked up a Burberry handbag from beside her and fumbled inside it, bringing out a key with an ident attached. She passed it to me.

'That's the key, Janie insisted I had one just in case – just in case of what I don't know. The address is on the tab. There's an alarm system, the keypad is on the wall in the hall on the right as you go in – it's 210666, my birthday. It's the only way I would ever remember the code.' She laughed to herself softly.

I had other questions, but I'd ask Harry later. I didn't want to overload Marcia Johnson's brain with nasty thoughts that her daughter may have been kidnapped or even murdered. I didn't really know why I was thinking along those lines either, but in my game you do, you just do.

'Okay.' I stood to go. 'I'll get round to the flat sometime today or in the morning and get a few things going, put a few feelers out. Hopefully Janie will turn up and wonder what all the fuss is about.' I gave Marcia Johnson a reassuring smile.

'Oh, I do hope so,' She did some more fumbling in the handbag, pulling out a card that she passed over. 'My home address and phone, Mr Nevis, please keep me informed, and please find her.'

I bade the pair of them goodbye and called an Uber to get home. I didn't fancy the walk back; it was beginning to rain and my Quo T-shirt would probably run – it was a knock-off from East Street market. I gave the Gold Digger a call from the cab.

'You working?' She sounded out of breath.

'No, at the gym.'

'Marcia Johnson mean anything to you?'

A short pause. 'Actress, good one – must be getting on a bit now, but if she was in it, you could bet it would be good. Did all those upstairs downstairs big-house-in-the-country dramas on TV.'

'The ones where the Duke's son gets the maid up the duff and she's sent away, and in the end the child inherits it all and the nasty grandparents end up potless?' I said. I can't stand them. The Gold Digger and me have totally different tastes in entertainment. She lives in BBC4 and Sky Arts; I live in Netflix and Sky Sports.

She laughed. 'Yes, why are you interested in her?'

'Harry Cohen called me in to meet her earlier. Her daughter's gone missing.'

'Didn't know she had one. How old?'

'Twenty-two – actress, good-looking.'

'Old enough to look after herself then.'

'Yeah, I thought that too.'

'So why is mummy so concerned?'

'You tell me. Have a dig around on the family background when you get a minute. I've got a few more questions that I didn't want to ask Harry in front of mummy – I'm going to give him a call.'

'Okay, I'll see what I can find out. You in the office tomorrow?'

'Yes.'

'I'll come round about ten.'

Click, she rang off. Not one for long goodbyes is the Gold Digger.

My first meeting with the Gold Digger – I just call her Gold – was in Pakistan in 2011 when I was with the military in N14, a part of the SAS. We were shadowing the US Seals as they took out Bin Laden's compound; our job was to intercept any Pakistan forces that might make for the area after the attack went in. They didn't, but a malfunction on one of the SEAL's Chinooks meant we picked up a few of them to lighten the payload. Gold was in the other shadow, an Israeli attack helicopter; at the time she was in a unit of Mossad's FB13 elite unit as a commander. We crossed paths at the debriefing after the operation and went our separate ways; I served the allowed time in N14 and was seconded into MI6 on the Anti-Terrorism Squad, and she left FB13 and went back to Mossad before her time was up too. In all the elite fighting forces of the world, your time in service is limited; keeps the units refreshed and you from getting stale, and making a mistake that could kill you and others.

After three years behind the Taliban lines, sometimes hidden less than five yards from one of their armed patrols, I wasn't too disappointed to be discarded and moved to MI6 – not too disappointed at all. A few years in MI6 and I got bored with shadowing Islamists and white supremacists and struck out with my own private investigator business. I reckoned that at forty-three if I didn't do it now, I never would. Gold meanwhile had put military service behind her too and moved to London and taken up gold digging again – the ancient art of a young lady relieving an older man of their wealth, or at least some of it, by giving the mark the impression she is about to surrender herself to his every whim. She never does, of course, and the old fool showers her with gifts and money in the false hope that they will unlock the door. At thirty-four I suppose Gold comes under the category of MILF, although she's not a mother – five eight and a tight slim figure belies her age. She reminds me of a young Jennifer Rush – younger readers, look JR up. 'Power of Love', one of the best ballads ever made.

Gold is very good at the gold digging scam, but made one mistake: she targeted one of my clients. I sussed it was a scam straight away, and when I set up a false meeting at the client's luxury home in Berkshire I couldn't believe who turned up. We clicked again and from then on she's been my back-up, hovering in the background watching my back when I'm working. Some of my 'jobs' involve nasty characters to whom violence is pretty standard procedure, so having Gold around limits the danger.

I made the call to Harry Cohen after I got home and made a coffee – a proper coffee – and had suppressed my hunger with a hot pork and apple sauce sandwich bought from the deli opposite. Lovely.

Harry's secretary answered.

'I've got the test results back – it's pink. Congratulations, now we'll have to get married.'

'Hold the line, Ben, I'll put you through.' Perhaps I'd played that line on her too many times. Harry's phone rang twice before he picked it up.

'Harry Cohen.'

'Ben Nevis, got a minute?'

'Yes, go on. What did you think of Marcia?'

'Lovely lady, bad situation.'

'Yes, I'm relying on you, Ben. Find the kid.'

Kid, she's twenty-two. 'Couple of questions, Harry, ones I didn't really want ask her.'

'Okay, fire away.'

'Where's the bill going?'

'To me.'

And I bet he takes his twenty percent before passing it to Marcia Johnson.

'Two grand a week or part of, plus expenses.'

'Okay.'

'Upfront.'

'Don't worry, Ben, she's good for it.'

'Upfront.' Business is business, and in the unlikely event that I don't find Janie, Marcia might not want to pay. Things don't always work out to the client's satisfaction, no matter how much time and effort you put in, and time and effort have to be paid for.

'All right, I'll transfer the first week to your bank account tomorrow. Next question?'

'Where's the husband?'

'Whose, Marcia's?'

'Yes. Where's her husband and Janie's father? She never mentioned him.'

'They split when Janie was three.

'Why?'

There was a silence for a few seconds. 'She kicked him out.'

'Why?'

'She was young and impressionable at the time, Ben, but not at the start of her career – already a *name*, and that sort of puts suitors off. You'll be playing second fiddle from the start, so not many chaps had the balls to date her except him.' Another pause. 'His name was James Randall.'

I could see why he had paused. 'THE James Randall?'

'Yes, THE James Randall.'

'He's dead.'

****

I finished the call and clicked on my laptop and pulled up James Randall on Wikipedia. I wanted to refresh my memory.

James Randall, London organised crime gang boss 1946 -2020. Eldest son of the Randall Crime family from South London. Controlled the London area drug scene with an estimated ton of cocaine sold every week through a network of street dealers and club security people. Established import routes directly from Costa Rica through Romania and Eastern Europe. Shot dead by Metropolitan Police Organised Crime Squad marksmen in Epping Forest after picking up bags of drugs dropped from a low flying Cessna aircraft and firing at police detectives.

And that was it? Nothing about his family, nothing about Marcia or Janie? Very strange. Had it been edited? You can do that with Wikipedia; if you have something to add to a post you can register as an editor and add it. I checked the page's editors. There it was – Harry Cohen edited the page March 2020. Harry had removed any reference to James Randall's marriage to Marcia and of their child Janie – all gone. It doesn't actually say what changes Harry had made, but it doesn't take much to figure it out. I skipped to Marcia Johnson's page. Same thing, Harry Cohen had been in and edited it. Pound to a penny he'd removed all reference to James Randall. But why?

Maybe producers and casting agents had been reluctant to look at Marcia Johnson for a part in their upcoming productions when she was married to James Randall, with the unspoken threat that if she didn't get the role they might get a visit? Now he was dead he could be removed from her life totally, and Harry had seen to that, so maybe he was thinking it would be good for Marcia's career. Janie didn't have a page.

Could there be a connection between James Randall and Janie's disappearance? Probably not; he was in her life a long while ago. I thought about taking a trip to Janie's flat but decided to wait until Gold was with me. She was more likely to pick up anything out of the ordinary in a girl's flat than I was. So I took a long hot shower and settled back to watch *The Irishman* on Netflix for the second time. Seeing Pesci and De Niro's large pictures on Harry Cohen's wall had reminded me of it. I love that film.

CHAPTER 2

210666 worked fine. The alarm box in the hall of Janie Johnson's flat beeped twice and the red LED went green.

I'd met Gold at the office and we took a cab to the address on the key fob Marcia had given me. Turned out to be a nice house in a small street off the Fulham Palace Road. One day I'll visit the Palace itself and wander round the museum. I'm sure tourists visit more of the interesting places in London than Londoners ever do – strange that. The house had been converted into ground and upper floor flats; Janie's was the upper. She'd kept it nice – four good-sized rooms, front lounge, bedroom, kitchen and bathroom.

Gold pulled pairs of paper overshoes and gloves from her shoulder bag and we put them on. Maybe we'd find a body, and I didn't want any crime scene contaminated by my size elevens.

'Right, I'll take the kitchen, you take the bedroom and bathroom. Meet in the lounge.'

The kitchen was spotless. Janie was obviously house-proud; no crockery left in the sink to be washed and the washing machine was empty, as was the waste bin. I stooped level with the granite worktops and looked along them; a very light covering of dust, enough to show nobody had wiped them for a few days. I checked all the drawers and cupboards; everything was in its rightful place. I moved into the lounge. A sofa covered with scatter cushions, two armchairs, a coffee table and a desk. Minimalistic. I checked down the back of the sofa cushions; a twenty pence piece, a toffee wrapper, and a few crumbs. I've had better. Gold came in.

'Anything?' I asked.

'No, the bed is made and everything tidy and in its place.'

'Okay.' I went over to a desk by the front windows and opened the drawers. They were obviously Janie's office; papers arranged in folders, all very neat. I pulled them out and spread them on the coffee table. We started going through them. Janie had kept her bills in order, just the usual utilities.

'She might have a cleaner.' Gold passed me a paper. West London Cleaning Company, Commercial and Residential Cleaning. It was a flyer advertising their services.

'Three hundred a month for a quick flit with a duster and washing up?'

Gold waved my remark away. 'Never mind that, we need to find out if she uses them and when they came in last. Give them a call.'

Gold was covering all the bases; if Janie had cancelled the cleaner then she obviously knew she was going away and was probably sunning herself on some hot beach in the Mediterranean. If she hadn't cancelled, then that made her disappearance suspicious.

****

West London Cleaning Company were closed down. I gave them a ring from the office the next morning but the phone was dead, so nothing worthwhile there.

What was bugging me was that Janie disappeared so soon after her father's death. Was there a connection, and if so what?

Gold came into the office but she hadn't turned up anything interesting. 'They never got a divorce, the BMD has still got them registered as married. Can you believe that all those years separated and Marcia never got a divorce?'

'That's strange. Perhaps she didn't want to go through all the publicity – she was a major star at the time.' I walked over to the front window and looked down on Borough High street, 'I can't help thinking James Randall has something to do with this Janie disappearance.'

'He's dead, and Harry Cohen said he'd been out of Janie's life for twenty years.'

'Yes, but only recently dead. What if Janie was in touch with him?'

‘And not telling her mum?’

‘Wouldn’t be the first time that daughters did things behind their mother’s backs.’

‘I find it more suspicious that Marcia hasn’t called in the police. I would think that’s the first thing a mother would do in these circumstances.’

I went back to the desk and sat down. ‘So why wouldn’t she?

‘And why would Harry Cohen advise her not to?

I shook my head. ‘I don’t know, bad publicity?’

‘Who, for Marcia? Her career’s basically over – might even give her name a boost in the public’s eyes.’

‘So why don’t people call in the police then?’

‘Fear.’

‘Fear?’

‘Marcia’s been told not to.’

‘Why?’

‘I don’t know. Could be Janie’s a hostage.’

‘A hostage?’ Where was Gold going with this?

‘She could have got mixed up in something to do with Randall and it’s gone pear-shaped.’

‘And Marcia knows?’

‘Yes, and she’s confided in Cohen who wants to keep the police out of it for some reason, and so he calls you.’

I opened the desk drawer and took out the piece of paper with Marcia Johnson’s address and phone number on and looked at it.

‘Fancy a trip to Hampstead?’

‘You drive, I’m not driving across London. It’s starting to rain and the traffic will pile up.’

‘Nor am I.’ I called an Uber.

CHAPTER 3

Marcia Johnson's house in Hampstead reflected a career earning top dollar. A large fake Tudor-style 1940s build set behind gates, and surrounded by well-kept gardens. She looked pleased to see me, even though I was unannounced. I told her I didn't have any good news and just wanted some more information. I introduced Gold and we followed her through a large open hall with a winding wide staircase leading up from it to the upper storey, through into a rear lounge which had French doors that would open onto a well-maintained garden in better weather. A late middle-aged man was standing looking out of them. By his work clothes I took him to be the gardener.

Marcia introduced us. 'This is Mr Layton, he looks after the gardens for me and keeps the house in decent repair. Houses are a bit like people, aren't they? The older they get, the more maintenance they need. George, this is Mr Nevis and Miss Gold. I told you about how he is helping me find Janie.'

George Layton held out a hand. 'Nice to meet you, Miss Gold – and you, Mr Nevis.'

Gold gave him a perfunctory nod as I took his hand. 'It's Ben.'

Layton raised his eyebrows. 'Ben Nevis, is that for real?'

'Yes, and it's a long story before you ask.'

'I already explained your name to George, Mr Nevis, just as Harry explained it to me. Do sit down.' She waved us towards a sofa and armchairs – four of them, which I thought was overdoing it a bit, but it was a large room. We took the sofa. 'Tea, coffee, cake?'

'Just eaten thank you, Mrs Johnson.'

'I'll leave you to it then.' George opened one of the French doors. 'Looks like the rain has eased off so I'll carry on with the garden. Nice to meet you both.' He gave a nod and stepped out, shutting the door behind him.

'Well then, how can I help you?' Marcia gave a false smile and perched on one of the armchairs opposite us, very prim and straight-backed, hands clasped in lap; straight out of the RADA handbook.

I started slowly with a soft smile. 'We've been to your daughter's flat and there's nothing there out of the ordinary, nothing out of place – nothing to suggest she'd been taken against her will.'

When we were in Harry Cohen's large office Marcia Johnson hadn't said anything about going to her daughter's flat herself, but she had no doubt been there – of course she had, first place you'd go if you were worried about your daughter and hadn't heard from her for a while. I passed the keys across to her, having had a copy set made at Timpson's when I'd left Cohen's. 'One thing that worries me, Mrs Johnson, is why you didn't call the police?'

'I was going to, but Harry thought it was too early to call them in. Janie could walk in at any time, and I'd look foolish and have wasted their time.'

'It had been a fortnight. No contact for a fortnight? I find it strange he would advise that.'

She sat motionless. Something told me I had hit pay dirt, so I continued. 'I think we should call them now, get Janie's description out.'

Marcia Johnson took a deep breath and sat for a moment; tears were filling her eyes. She shook her head slowly from side to side.

'I can't.'

'You can't? You can't what, call the police?''

'Yes.' She rose from her chair and fetched an envelope from the drawer of a side table and offered it to me.

Gold was ahead of the game and stayed my hand with hers. 'Wait.' She opened her shoulder bag and pulled out a pair of paper gloves and gave them to me. I put them on, took the envelope, opened it and pulled out a single sheet of paper. It was the same West London Cleaners flyer that was in Janie's drawer at the flat, only this one had a message handwritten on the back:

YOU GET HER BACK WHEN WE GET OURS BACK

Marcia Johnson sat down again. 'That was on the kitchen table when I went round to Janie's flat.'

'What does it mean, do you know?' I asked her.

'No.' She shook her head in despair. 'I've no idea – if I did then whatever it is they want I'd give it to them.'

'Did you show this to Harry?'

'Yes.'

So, a distraught mother, a '*national treasure*' and an old friend had gone to Harry Cohen with a ransom note for the return of her daughter, and Harry had called a private eye. He hadn't called the police, and more to the point he hadn't told me about the note. Why was he so intent on keeping the police out of it? I thought Harry Cohen deserved another visit.

'May I keep this?' I asked, holding up the envelope and paper.

'Of course.'

'I'll get it tested for fingerprints.'

'Thank you.'

'Have you had any more thoughts as to why Janie has disappeared? Anything she did out of the ordinary? Any people she mentioned that she'd seen or was going to see?

'No, none.' The tears were beginning fall slowly down her face. 'I feel so useless, Mr Nevis, so damn useless.'

'Well don't feel like that, Mrs Johnson, you're not in any way useless. I need you here as a sort of base. If your daughter has been kidnapped, then the kidnapper or kidnappers will send their demands to you. That message was left at Janie's flat for *you* to find. When they realise that you have no idea what they are talking about, I would think they'll come back and make it plain. In the meantime, Gold and I will start our enquiries.' That sounded all very professional and comforting, but my enquiry methods can be far from professional or comforting, as Harry Cohen would find out soon enough.

We stood and made our way to the front door.

'You're the first private investigator I've met, Mr Nevis.'

'You're lucky, Mrs Johnson, the other ones aren't so good-looking.'

I brought a smile to her face. We took our leave.

CHAPTER 4

The silence in the Uber that took us to Harry Cohen's was shattering.

I know the way Gold works and she was sitting in the back, deep in thought and Googling on her iPhone. Any interruption would have been met with total silence and ignored. At Cohen's we stood outside in Wardour Street; thankfully the rain had stopped.

'Well?' I asked. 'What are you thinking?'

'I'm thinking that whoever has Janie obviously thinks her mother knows exactly what they want in exchange for her safe return. But I don't think Marcia does know – her body language was despair, not understanding. She's no idea what this is all about, and the words 'ours' in the note indicates it's a group who have her. Why wouldn't they ask for money? If it was a straight kidnap for ransom they would. Whatever it is they want has a bigger value than money, or it's part of something that needs to be got back. Marcia Johnson doesn't, as far as we know, associate with people who do kidnaps.' She stopped and looked me straight in the eye with her eyebrows raised, waiting for my input.

'But James Randall did.' I could see where Gold was going with this.

'Exactly.'

'He's dead.'

'Killed by police marksmen six months ago after picking up a consignment of drugs in Epping Forest.'

'Mmm.' I nodded.

'Nothing in any of the news reports that I've researched say anything about the drugs being seized by the police. No mention as to how big a shipment Randall was collecting. Nothing about him having an accomplice with him, and if he did was he shot too, or did he get away with the drugs?'

I was catching up to speed on Gold's thoughts. 'Randall shifted tons of cocaine – he wouldn't have had a plane drop a load in Epping Forest if it wasn't a worthwhile amount, and he definitely wouldn't go alone.'

'Quite, so where is it? Is it that load that our kidnappers think Marcia knows the whereabouts of? And what relationship did they have with Randall?'

'Or maybe Randall hadn't paid for it and somebody wants their money.' I thought for a moment. 'Okay, change of plan. You go back to the office and hassle your newspaper contacts and see if we can't get more info on the Epping Forest thing. I'm going to have a chat with an old mate of mine at Organised Crime and get the police side of the story.

See you back at the office when I'm done. Get a cab, looks like more rain coming.'

Gold hailed a cab as I checked the phone book on my mobile and pressed Dick Clancy's number. He picked up on the second ring.

'Clancy.'

'Is that Clancy of the Yard?'

'What do you want, Nevis?' He sounded pissed off at me before I'd even asked a favour.

'Are you in?'

'Not if you're coming over, no.'

'Ten minutes of your time could rescue a maiden in distress.'

'If she's mixed up with you, Nevis, she's definitely in distress.'

'Fourth floor West End Central?'

'Yes, and ten minutes maximum. I'll put your name at the door.'

Click.

Dick Clancy had worked with me in my time in the London Organised Crime Squad. The office is on the fourth floor of West End Central Police Station in Savile Row. I decided to walk there as the rain hadn't materialised; didn't take long from Wardour street and pretty soon I was negotiating the anti-terrorist car bomb concrete bollards shielding the front entrance, to be patted down and told to sign the visitor's book and show some ID. My driving licence in my wallet did the trick. I took the stairs to the fourth floor – more interesting than the inside of a steel lift; you could be nosy and see inside the open plan offices on each floor, check out the mug shots pinned on the case progress boards, see if mine and Gold's were there – I'm joking! Didn't seem to be a lot going on; lots of empty desks, probably all out trying to keep a lid on the muggers and street corner dealers that populate the West End these days. No chance of winning that battle, unless you trebled the number of officers on the streets.

DCS Clancy was sitting at his desk. His door was open and I gave it a knock as I went in.

'It says knock and *wait.*'

'Yeah, but I know how you can't wait to see me. Wetting yourself with excitement'

'Whatever you want make it quick.'

I pulled the envelope with the ransom note inside from my pocket and placed it in front of him. 'I'd like the note inside to be checked for prints, and any prints run through the system.'

'Why? And who's the maiden in distress you mentioned on the phone?'

I sat on one of two empty chairs in front of his desk and ran through the whole case so far. When I'd finished, Clancy sat back and took a deep breath. 'If you are getting involved in the circles James

Randall moved in you need to be very careful, Ben – very careful indeed.'

He doesn't usually call me Ben, so I must have hit on a raw nerve. I pressed further. 'What happened to the drugs he was picking up?'

He shrugged. 'You tell me, the official story is that his accomplice got away with them.'

'Nothing about an accomplice in the news media reports.'

'Randall wouldn't have done a job like that on his own – he always had backup. In the level of dealing he was in, Ben, you needed it – threat level high was how I'd describe his life.'

'Okay, so what happened – did the other guy get away with the load? Come on, Dick, a specialist AR marksmen unit wouldn't let anybody get away.'

'What are you suggesting?'

'If there was an accomplice with Randall he was let go on purpose, with or without the load.'

'Why?'

'Because he was the one who gave the OC a heads-up on the drop time and place.'

'And the load went with him?'

'Maybe, or maybe not. It went with somebody.'

'Careful, Ben.' Clancy could see where I was going with this.

'I know, I know, but Randall wouldn't generally pick up a load himself, would he? So this one must have been special – a very big one, maybe? We know he moved a large quantity of charlie every week through his dealers, so perhaps this was a special one-off. Think about it, Dick, he wouldn't have a plane come in and take a chance to drop just a couple of bricks, current price twenty-three grand a kilo, so if the drop was, say, fifty bricks, that's a million plus – that's a lot of dosh split four ways. Three is the usual number of marksmen in an OC Marksman Unit isn't it, Dick? Plus the grass makes four?'

Clancy bristled. 'Careful, Ben – if you start throwing those kind of accusations around, you could be in serious trouble. How does this fit in with the missing girl?'

'I don't know, but I'll hazard a guess that whoever that load of coke came from hasn't been paid and wants their money or the drugs back. They must think Randall was still married to Marcia Johnson and she's part of his business and has the money stashed somewhere, or at least knows where it is. I can't think of any other reason to take the girl.'

Clancy crossed his arms, body language for building a wall. He didn't like me bringing his own men into play. 'I'm not going to go there, Ben. I'm not opening the file and I'm not going to ask questions.' He paused. 'Officially, that is – unofficially I will take a look at the officers' statements, but if this lady walks back in tomorrow and wonders what all the fuss is about, that file closes and you forget it, understood? I've enough on my plate without re-opening shut cases without a cast iron reason. Put the girl on a missing persons list – if anything nasty happens to her, questions will be asked as to why you didn't. I'll call you if any prints on the note match anyone on the database. Now bugger off and let me work.'

'One last thing you might help me with.'

Clancy sighed and raised his eyes to the Heavens. 'Go on.'

'What happened with Randall's gang after he was killed?'

'What happened to them?'

'Yes, did they split up or are they still going with another boss?'

'There was only three of them, Ben. Randall was a wholesaler – bought from producers in bulk, split it, and sold it on to the postcode and county line gangs. He didn't get mixed up in the street end of things.'

'So what happened to the other two?'

'Moved in with the Romanians.'

'Romanians?'

'Yes, most of Randall's business was with them. They're the biggest players now, Ben – when Romania joined the EU it gave them free travel into the UK, and the Romanian drug gangs took full advantage of it. Nasty people, violence is second nature to them. Now we are out of Europe hopefully it will stem the influx, but they're very well-established here now. We have a unit monitoring them – clever people.'

A name came to my mind. 'Alexandru Bogdan, is he still the top man?' I'd had a couple of run ins with him over the last few years; nasty piece of work, blew up one of my client's nightclubs when the client wouldn't employ Bogdan's security people on the door. If you're dealing drugs and get your people on a nightclub door, they control who gets in and make sure only your dealers do. Big money changes hands between dealers and door staff; big, big money.

'You know Bogdan?' Clancy was surprised.

'Oh yes, I know Alexandru Bogdan.' I'd taken out the two goons he'd sent to teach me a lesson after the nightclub episode. I don't take prisoners, and I don't leave bodies lying around; no bodies means no evidence. I have a couple of contacts, twins in fact, who work at a south London crematorium and are open to a bit of after-hours overtime, and a few fifty pound notes in a brown envelope. I call them my magicians – why magicians? Because they make things disappear, especially bodies.

Clancy pursed his lips and gave me a serious look. 'Well, if you know Bogdan you don't need me to tell you to be careful.'

We shook hands and I left.

****

Gold wasn't impressed. 'Do you really want to ignite the flames of that battle? Bogdan knows you disappeared two of his men so he's not likely to welcome you with open arms if you start digging into his business – and you don't even know that he's involved.'

We were having a sandwich at the concourse cafe at Charing Cross station. We meet there when a case is ongoing; simple reason is that if there is anybody involved that wants us out of the picture they would be looking for us at my office, so we give it a miss. The concourse cafe at Charing Cross is ideal; a window seat gives a full view of anybody approaching. The food's okay, but stay away from the British Rail coffee – there's no known antidote.

Gold continued, 'If Randall's men moved across to Bogdan and now work for him, where's the reason for him to take Janie? If they or one of them got away with the drugs from Epping Forest, Bogdan would have them.'

'What if he hasn't got them? What if Randall was bringing them in for Bogdan, and Bogdan had paid upfront and *didn't* get them? He'd want his money back.'

'And he thinks Marcia Johnson has it?

'Why not? She was his wife, and there was no divorce, so he probably thinks they are still together. So why not?'

'So he thinks Marcia has the coke or the money.'

'Or both if the drop was made.'

'She's in a pretty bad position, isn't she.'

'Which is one good reason to go and talk to Bogdan.'

My mobile buzzed.

'You've reached Ben Nevis Private Investigations, how may we help you?' Corny, eh? But every other company says 'How may we help you' and then proceeds not to. I'm different; I usually do.

A sombre voice said, 'Detective Sergeant Ansty, Hampstead crime squad. You know Marcia Johnson?'

'Yes.' I was worried what would come next.

'She says you're working for her, is that right?'

Well, at least she's not dead.

'Yes, that's right.'

'You'd better get over here to her house then. She's had a break-in and taken a beating.'

'I'm on my way.'

****

You know when you see the bruised faces of elderly people who have been mugged on the TV News you get angry inside? Well that's how I felt when I saw Marcia Johnson's face – more blue than pink.

DS Ansty had met me at the door. Old school copper, mid-fifties, heavy build, receding hairline, expanding stomach; seen it all and didn't take prisoners. Marcia's house was swarming with white paper-suited forensic officers. I put on a pair of overshoes and followed Ansty into the lounge, where Marcia sat on the sofa next to a victim support officer and a man I took to be her doctor by the stethoscope hanging round his neck. She looked relieved to see me. I couldn't see any result of a break-in; everything was as I remembered it. Nothing broken, no drawers emptied over the floor, the French door glass unbroken.

'You okay?' Stupid question, but what else should I say?

She gave me a smile. 'I think so, nothing broken.' She managed a weak smile.

'What's your relationship with Mrs Johnson?' Ansty was asking. Ansty was suspicious.

'Her daughter's gone missing, I'm trying to find her.'

'Is she on the missing persons list?'

'No.'

'Really?' Ansty arched his eyebrows.

I thought quickly. 'Bearing in mind Mrs Johnson's public persona, her agent thought it best to have a low key look for her first. She may have just gone away for a break and forgotten to tell anybody. Put it on missing persons and the press would be all over it.'

'Did you agree with that, Mrs Johnson?' Ansty asked.

Marcia nodded. 'Yes, my daughter is twenty-two, not a slip of a girl. I'm sure she's probably just done what Mr Nevis said, gone on holiday or something and not told me, that's all. Probably walk in any minute. Not worth taking up police time.'

Ansty looked at me. 'You agree?'

'No, but I'm the hired help, not the client.' I changed the subject. 'I thought you said it was a break-in? Nothing seems out of place.'

'Yes, strange, isn't it?' Ansty was giving me that suspicious look again. 'Mrs Johnson says two men came to the door – foreigners – bundled her in here and one stayed with her whilst the other searched the house.'

'Searched for what?'

'You tell me, Nevis. It was a professional search, gloves worn and everything left in order – nothing chucked on the floor, nice and clean. So what were they looking for?' His eyes pinned me down.

'No idea. Probably a pair of random chancers taking a punt?'

'And leaving Mrs Johnson's jewellery untouched on the dressing table in her bedroom? The *foreigners* bit is unusual. If they were a pair of illegals after money, they'd have taken the jewellery to sell on. No, these were pros, and they were after something specific. I reckon you know more than you are saying, Nevis.' The look I got was made of granite.

Thankfully the forensic boss poked his head round the door to say they'd finished and were off. Ansty would get a report in a day or two, but there wouldn't be much to it. And that was that. Mrs Johnson was to go to the local police station tomorrow to make a statement and look through the mugshots of known local ne'er-do-wells, in the forlorn hope she might recognise someone. Not a hope in Hell. Maybe a file of known felons from the Politia Romana would offer a better chance. It was time I had a chat with Alexandru Bogdan; I was moving into dangerous territory, but there wasn't any alternative now.

I left the same time as Ansty and his officers; the doctor was still there but Marcia insisted she was fine and let the victim support officer go. I wanted to get some more information out of Marcia, but not in front of Ansty. I'd call her when I got home.

I didn't get that far. Mrs Johnson rang me five minutes after I'd left and asked me to go back.

She was at the door waiting and ushered me into the lounge, before pressing a photo into my hand.

'They gave me this.' Her voice was shaky.

The photo was of Janie. She was blindfolded and stood against a brick wall, hands tied behind her.

'They spoke English, asked where it was.'

'It?'

'Yes, I said what are you talking about and they said I knew. I said I didn't, and one hit me a couple of times and asked again, '*where is it?*'. I said I didn't know what they were talking about, and one went off to search the house and the other kept slapping my face demanding to know where *it* was, and if I didn't tell him I'd never see Janie again.' She broke down in tears. 'What should I do, Mr Nevis, what should I do? I rang Harry and he said to ask you, but don't show the photo to the police because the kidnappers might harm her if the police are involved.'

I calmed her down and told her she was quite safe. If the goons had been and found nothing they wouldn't be back, and they'd be pretty sure Marcia Johnson had no idea what they were after or she would have crumbled at the sight of the photo and given it up.

I haven't any kids. I haven't met anybody I'd want to have them with-yet. Been near to settling with a couple of ex's in the past, but it always collapsed. I'd be a great dad, I really would; I could see myself at the school gates picking them up. I'd be a rock for them, the sort of dad I never had: caring, understanding, a chaperone or a best mate. I wouldn't care if it was a boy or girl; I can glare at a daughter's first boyfriends as they threatened to usurp my throne, or have a quiet word with the king of the block about what would happen to him if my son got involved in his little drug-selling game. Yes, I'd be a good dad. Is Marcia Johnson a good mum? The jury's out.

I needed to have a one-to-one chat with Harry Cohen; he seemed a bit too keen to keep the police out of it, a bit too keen by far. But first Alexandru Bogdan would receive my attention. Alexandru is the eldest of five brothers who run their organised crime family from Bucharest. The father, now retired, started it all with the black market in the war, then progressed into drugs and people trafficking which are much more lucrative and profitable.

****

I dressed for the occasion: stab-proof vest and my Beretta M9, with a full clip tucked into my belt behind me. I'd screwed on the silencer. I rang Gold.

'You busy?'

'No, just cloning a debit card that one of my clients accidently dropped into my shoulder bag.'

Sometimes I don't know whether or not to believe Gold.

'I'm going to Bogdan's place. Marcia Johnson had a couple of visitors earlier.'

'Really? She okay?'

'Bit shook up, but listen to this – two foreigners who tossed the place, but left it as tidy as they found it.'

Gold thought for a moment. 'The ransom note didn't work, so a visit was made then?'

'Yes, I think so. They had a picture of Janie, bound and gagged.'

'Putting the pressure on.'

'Yeah, big time.'

'Gotta be something big they're after.'

'I'm sure Mr Bogdan will know, he wouldn't be involved for peanuts. I'm going to their club, can you watch my back?'

'Club Bucharest?'

'Yes.'

'Straight into the lion's den, eh?'

'I'll get an answer.'

'You might get a beating.'

'Can you cover my back? I'll be there about eleven.'

'Of course. Oh, by the way, I did some digging on George Layton. He's got a record, three offences listed.'

'He has?' Was this the break we were looking for?

'Exceeding the speed limit in a 30mph area, three of them.'

'Not exactly what I was hoping for.' I was a bit disappointed.

'Well, one of them may have been exceeding the speed limit whilst fleeing Epping

Forest.' Gold has a dry wit. 'I'll be at the Bucharest by eleven.'

I felt better knowing Gold would be around. My silent partner, always lurking in the background and ready to step in when needed.

CHAPTER 5

The Bogdans' 'Bucharest Club' was off Commercial Road, East London, a place you were welcome if they knew you and told you in no uncertain language where to go if they didn't. A place where illegal deals of all sorts were agreed behind the facade of a big and busy night club, and where it had been known people went in and never came out. The Commercial Road was aptly named in the 1800s when it was a dock land centre for merchant sailors on leave from ships berthed in the docks nearby to find prostitutes, and get waylaid by muggers and a fair selection of people you really didn't want to meet on a dark, unlit road at night staggering back to your ship with a belly full of beer and jellied eels. Then the developers moved in around the 1960s and the tall warehouses that loomed over the street became executive apartments with river views sitting on top of posh bistros and restaurants with the occasional nightclub.

I'd sorted out a few dodgy deals on behalf of clients with the Bogdans in the past, when those clients had painted themselves into a corner with silly demands and needed a little oil spread on the choppy waters to get the deal done and them out in one piece. You don't make threats to the Bogdan family; even the Romanian police learnt that lesson when they went to arrest two of the five brothers and ended up with three of their squad dead and no arrests. In his younger days Alexandru, the eldest brother, was known in Romania as '*the widow maker*' – no prizes for guessing why.

I booked an Uber to take me and got out, knowing that the eyes of the doormen were on me. Both of them were old faces I knew, standing motionless and expressionless, their over-long black Crombie coats flapping slowly in the soft breeze, checking handbags of the girls going in and frisking the boys. There was a big queue; the club was popular. Only Bogdan family coke would be lined and snorted inside. A captive market.

I smiled at the biggest doorman. 'Hello, Tony. Thought you were past all this, thought you'd be sitting on a beach in Bermuda by now?'

Tony Capp gave me a cold smile. 'Big Tony' was as black as the ace of spades, six foot-high and just about the same in breadth. The size of his shoulders stretched the Crombie fabric to the limit and his shaved head sat like a dome in the middle of them. Tony had no neck; a head and chest, but nothing in between – it was there, of course, but hidden in fat and muscle. His partner on the door was the same height but slim; slicked back jet-black hair and a trimmed top lip moustache, one of Bogdan's imported Romanian goons. Probably on the door because the club had a large Eastern European membership, and unless 'Big Tony' had been to evening classes, his language skills rated zero.

'Ben Nevis,' he said without expression. 'What are you doing here?'

'Got an appointment with Alexandru.'

'Yeah?'

'Yeah.'

He stepped to the side where a phone hung, pressed a button and spoke. Bad decision, Tony – now I knew Alexandru was inside the building. I walked past the pair of them, which caused alarm on their faces. 'Big Tony' dropped the phone which hung and swung against the wall and ran at me. I knew that if those arms got around me I'd have no chance; a bear hug from Tony would push the air from my lungs like a burst balloon, and probably snap a couple of ribs at the same time. I reached behind me and pulled out my Beretta and shot him in the foot. He'd have a permanent limp, but wouldn't die. He pulled up and went down on one knee. I kicked him in the face, breaking his nose which streamed blood down the front of his Crombie; he was out of the game, but Mr Moustache was recovering from the shock and coming my way. I stepped forward to meet him; he was expecting me to back off, so was surprised for a moment. That moment was all I needed to bring the Beretta up hard under his chin. He slumped unconscious to the floor, a mixture of blood and broken teeth slipping from his open mouth.

There was pandemonium in the doorway and on the street, people falling over people as they fled the area. I walked through the doors into the main room; it was pretty dark, and the dance floor was packed with clubbers squashed together, vibrating to the loud decibels from the DJ booth that pumped through your body in time with the flashing strobe lights. The news of the fracas in the entrance hadn't got into the room; no panic, and the security men were stood against the walls. I counted four, with one stood outside a door marked: 'STAFF ONLY- PRIVATE'. That's where Alexandru would be.

I felt a tap on my shoulder and turned, moving my hand back to my gun. It was Gold, the strobe lights flashing across her face in the dark. I shouted into her ear, 'Move the bloke by the door,' and nodded towards him.

Gold left me and moved off into the crowded dance floor. I edged my way through towards the door. A fight broke out amongst the punters on the floor about five metres to the right of the door. Two females were arguing and then one hit the floor, and the other, Gold, started to kick her. The goon by the door was the nearest security to it and started to push his way through the crowd to sort it out. I took my chance and went through the door as fast as I could, pulling out the Beretta.

Inside Alexandru Bogdan was sitting behind a large desk reading a magazine; opposite him two goons sitting on a sofa playing pontoon dropped their cards and started to go for their shoulder holsters.

I put a bullet in the head of the nearest and in the arm of the other one, who cried in pain and slumped down onto the floor trying to stem the blood. I had one eye on Alexandru Bogdan, and when he reached to open a drawer at the desk he was sitting behind I put a bullet into the wall behind him, very, very close to his head.

'Don't even think about it.'

The goon on the floor decided to try and get to his shoulder holster with his good arm. Bad decision. His head jerked back against the sofa as the bullet went through it and into the furniture. 9mm bullets are powerful things; I've seen one go through two bodies and still bury itself three inches into a wall.

Bogdan was seeing sense and had slowly raised his hands above his head. I clicked the lock shut on the door to the club room and slid two heavy bolts across to secure it. The soundproofing was good, I couldn't hear a thing. With a bit of luck the news about the episode in the front would be getting through and security's attention moving there.

I moved beside Bogdan and held my gun to his head as I opened the drawer and took out a PKK Walther and put it in my belt.

'Do you know who I am?' I asked.

He was very calm. 'Yes, Ben Nevis – named after a racehorse, not a mountain.'

'Very good.'

'We have done business in the past, Mr Nevis, but not business like this. I seem to recall I sent two of my men to have a word with you some time ago. They still haven't come back. Perhaps they got lost?

'Perhaps.'

He shot a glance at his dead goons. 'What do you want?'

I pulled out the photo of Janie bound and gagged. 'I want her.'

'Aah, now I see. And what if I don't have her?'

'I'll kill you.'

'And what if I do have her?'

'I'll probably kill you anyway. Where is she?'

'I seem to remember you were a good negotiator, Mr Nevis. Perhaps we should negotiate?'

'You aren't in a good position to negotiate, Alexadru.'

'Then an offer, not a negotiation.'

'An offer?'

'Yes. The lady's father owes my family a million pounds sterling, did you know that? Unfortunately the goods he promised us for that million never materialised, and nor did the refund, and he died. In our business, Mr Nevis, family is everything, but the man's family have not refunded us. Now they will, or the daughter will disappear.'

'You're talking about James Randall and the Epping Forest delivery.'

'You are well informed. Yes I am, but it was not delivered – the police intercepted it.'

Not according to Dick Clancy they didn't. The firearms unit SCO19 had reported that Randall's accomplice had got away with the drugs. Perhaps Clancy needed to take a closer look at that operation. He said he would; I wondered if he'd come up with anything interesting?

'The police report says the driver got away with the drugs.'

'No, if he had he would have brought them to us, and if he had sold that amount to another dealer we would hear about it. No, the only way those drugs left the Forest was in a police vehicle. So I want my money back.'

Interesting, but this wasn't why I was here. 'The lady you sent the ransom note to and then had beaten up knows nothing about it.'

'Family, Mr Nevis, family. She is Randall's wife – she knows where my money is.'

'They divorced twenty years ago – the daughter you have kidnapped was three at the time and never knew her father. Marcia Johnson hasn't seen Randall for twenty years. She and the daughter have nothing to do with the money.'

'Perhaps you should have a word with Harry Cohen.'

Harry Cohen? What has he to do with this? I was getting confused.

'Harry Cohen the agent?' I asked.

'Yes, for the last ten years we have bought our merchandise from Randall in varying amounts to send out to Romania. The border police in the EU are very, very good – they have a good network, and we were losing many mules bringing it in, and our boats coming across the Black Sea were regularly stopped. We lost a lot of money, and others were taking our business. Randall had a good idea. Cohen sends his, what you call, '*boy bands*' out on tour round Europe using the same road crew each time. We used them – amplifiers stuffed with kilo bags of cocaine. They were never searched, works well. Randall got ninety percent of my family's business.'

'You still doing it?'

'Of course, but we buy our own product now and Mr Cohen handles the logistics.'

No wonder Harry Cohen didn't want the police involved.

The handle on the door turned, and the door shook as somebody put their shoulder against it. The lock and bolts held, and then there was thumping on the door; it wouldn't hold for long. There was another door in the side wall of the room. I had to act quickly before the goons came that way too. I fired twice at the door to the dance floor; the 9mms went straight through, and I hoped I'd hit a goon and not a punter. I had; the banging stopped. I released the spent magazine from the Beretta, took a new one from my pocket and pushed it in.

Bogdan was beginning to look worried. I pointed to the photo again.

'Where is she?'

'Not here.'

It wasn't the answer I wanted. 'Where?'

'You won't get out of here, no chance.' He gave a smile.

I'd had enough. I aimed the gun towards his groin. 'Where?'

'Somewhere you won't find her. You could work for me, Nevis – you get my money, I pay you a finder's fee, let the girl go, and we call it quits.'

I knew full well that my finder's fee would be a bullet in the head. I moved the gun slightly to the right and put a bullet in his left knee. 'Where?'

It sunk into his stupid brain that I meant business as he screamed in pain and fell sideways off his chair, squirming on the floor like footballers do when they feign a leg injury. I raised my gun and aimed at his other knee. 'Where?'

'Bucharest.'

'I don't believe you.'

'She is, at The Amsterdam Club – she is!' The pain he was in had brought out the truth. I couldn't see that anything Alexandru Bogdan would ever do in his life would add to the wealth of mankind's knowledge, so I put a bullet in his brain. No more widows.

I eased open the door on the sidewall. It led into a narrow corridor, obviously an escape route for Bogdan if needed. At the end of the corridor another door with a head-height glass window led into a room full of beer kegs and boxes of bottled drinks and bar snacks; I must be behind the bar. A door led off to the right, and by the sound coming through it must lead into the bar. Another door on the opposite wall must be for deliveries. I pushed on the security bar, opened the door slowly and stepped out into a side alley; it was wide enough for delivery vehicles. To the left the alley ended with a wall, high with razor wire on the top; to the right the alley skirted to the end of the building and came out on a side road. I speed-dialled Gold.

'You out?' I asked.

'Yes, sounded like you were having fun. Any survivors?'

'They weren't very helpful.'

'No survivors then.' She knows me so well.

'You in a motor?'

'Yes, where are you?'

'First left past the club, with the club on your left.'

'Okay.'

Click.

I hurried to the end of the alley and stood against the wall in the dark. Gold was there almost as soon as I was. No lights. I jumped in and we drove away.

'Home?' she asked.

'I think so.' I brought her up to speed on what I'd found out on the way.

CHAPTER 6

The next morning I left Gold at the front door to Harry's office to tell anybody coming in from the street that it was closed for the day. The secretary looked halfway between disappointed and bemused that I didn't offer a sexy quip on my through reception to Harry's office. I stopped at his door and looked back at her. 'No calls, he's in conference.'

Harry looked surprised to see me.

'Ben?' he asked as he took a pull on one of his large cigars in his hand. 'Everything okay with Marcia? Nasty state of affairs being attacked in your own house. How's she doing?'

A look of perceived fear crossed his face when I didn't take a seat and carried on round his large desk and stood very close beside him.

'She's okay. Want to tell me about Randall and Bogdan?'

'Who?'

Harry's mind must have been turning over at warp speed trying to work out what I knew and how to answer me. I didn't wait for it to settle. I snatched the large cigar from his hand, pushed his chair so it turned him to face me, held him steady by his tie and stubbed the cigar a few times on his forehead, sending burning tobacco flecks down his face, settling on his large neck. He squealed like a stabbed pig.

'Randall and Bogdan,' I asked again, and stubbed again. I was quite enjoying it – maybe I should get counselling?

'Okay, okay!' He was flapping his hands in surrender. I let go and sat half sideways on his large desk silently waiting, blowing softly on the cigar end to keep the leaves smouldering. 'When Marcia married Randall, he pressured me into helping get some drugs into Europe – started off small and then grew. I wanted out, but he threatened to tell the press and involve Marcia if I didn't go along with it. He introduced Bogdan to me as his partner. Everything went out inside the stage kit on the European tours.'

'You changed Marcia and Randall's Wikipedia entries after he died.'

'They updated it about his death and drug dealing, so I took anything about Marcia being his wife out of it, and I took anything about him out of her's – the media would have had a field day. With no divorce, to all intents and purposes they were still married. You can imagine the press feeding frenzy, she'd be ruined.'

'And you carried on with Bogdan.'

'I didn't have any choice, Ben. He could have me arrested and ruin my business with one tip-off to the police. People like him have friends in the law.

'So you knew that Bogdan has Janie all along.'

'Yes, he told me – he says Randall owes him back the money for the deal the police stopped, and Marcia must have it. I told him she's not involved, but he won't listen – says she's Randall's wife, so she must know where it is.'

'He won't trouble her again. He's dead.'

'What?'

'And you haven't seen me.' I got off the desk. 'You hear me? You haven't seen me.'

'Yes, yes.'

I left his office. The secretary looked at me.

'Everything all right?'

'If you've got anything for skin burns, he could use it.'

****

Gold dropped me back at home; I didn't want to go to the office as that's the first place the police would come looking. I'd be on the Bucharest Club CCTV, so no point in denying I was there.

Home is one of those converted warehouse executive apartments off the York road with views of the Thames that I bought when I left the Met. It's serviced and has door security officers, so nobody gets in without the okay from a resident. My apartment is pretty basic: lounge, kitchen and bedroom, with balcony looking over the Thames. As far as the council rates department are concerned, my name is George Hadlow, a name I got off a gravestone in a Great Plague cemetery in York Road; a friend of a friend of a friend made me up the appropriate ID, and that was it. So anybody trying to find where I live hits a wall. I have no home address.

I rang Marcia Johnson. She was okay; a neighbour had come in for the afternoon and chatted, but not about Janie she assured me. I told her she'd not be getting any more nasty visitors and to blank all contact with Harry Cohen, I'd explain why when I saw her. She didn't seem surprised. Perhaps she knew more than she was telling me?

I rang the air charter company I use at London City Airport and booked a flight to Debrecen airport in Hungary for the morning, the nearest airport to the Romanian border, I wasn't going to fly into Bucharest direct as no doubt the news of Alexandru's death would have reached the *family*, and they'd have put two and two together and linked it to Janie's kidnap and be watching the arrivals for me. Why me? Well, 'Big Tony' wouldn't be too happy with me leaving a bullet in his foot and would have named me, no doubt. Perhaps I should have put one in his head too. Am I getting soft?

I rang Gold and told her my plan.

'Okay, I'll get a flight into Bucharest tomorrow and sort out a place to stay, so keep a low profile until I call you.' Sometimes she's like a mother to me.

The next thing on the agenda was a gun. I didn't want to walk into the Bogdans' home turf unarmed, but both Hungary and Rumania have some of the toughest gun laws in Europe. I'd cross that bridge when I got there.

The evening news was full of pictures of what happened at the Bucharest Club the evening before, and vox-pops of clubbers giving their stories. I smiled at 'Big Tony' being stretchered into an ambulance and refusing to answer the reporters' questions being shouted at him; he didn't look happy. The anchor in the studio said the police had not commented, but it looked like gang warfare had broken out, probably drugs related. Well, they got that bit right. I turned my mobile off; Clancy would be after me like a pack of hounds on a hare when he got wind of it.

I took a stroll out later that evening and picked up a couple of Big Macs; I couldn't be bothered to cook and they're quite filling. Washed them down with a French style coffee, watched a bit of TV and went to bed. The charter flight was booked for late morning the next day, so I could get a good night's sleep after a good couple of days' work.

CHAPTER 7

I like flying. But I don't like flying crammed inside a steel tube with two hundred holidaymakers, and a snotty kid looking over the seat in front blowing bubbles with his nose – no, I don't like that at all. I'm not one for crowds; a deserted beach or windswept moor, yes – Bournemouth on Bank Holiday weekend, no. So a twelve-seater Cessna charter flight with no other passengers suited me just fine. The air charter company I use know me; they know I like privacy and they know I'm sometimes in a hurry to get into or out of a country. They also know I pay promptly.

There was a low cloud base over Europe so not much to see, but there's something very soothing about clouds and the pictures they make. Gold hates them; says she sees the faces of dead colleagues in them. I told her to let me know if she ever sees me. My soothing period was brought to an abrupt end by Clancy on my mobile. I'd only had it turned on for three minutes and there he was.

'What the Hell went on at the Bucharest Club, Nevis? You re-enacting the Gunfight at the OK Corral? The shit has really hit the fan now!' He was really angry.

'I had a disagreement with Bogdan.'

‘I told you we had a team watching him.’

‘Well, nobody to watch now.’

‘The Commissioner’s gone up the bloody wall and the Home Secretary is after blood!’

‘Should be some on the floor in Bogdan’s office.’

‘And you are all over the CCTV. Your office has been watched all night and the only thing stopping an international arrest warrant going out on you is me. Where are you?’

‘On a plane going to get the missing girl back – she’s in Romania. Bogdan took her because Randall owes him the money back for the Essex job. He paid upfront for the drugs and didn’t get them, he wants his money back and he thinks Marcia Johnson has it. He didn’t know they had separated twenty years ago.’

That set Clancy back on his heels for a few seconds. ‘Nor did I.’

‘The money’s gone – I don’t know where, but Bogdan wasn’t going to get it back and he’d take a lot of convincing. Next thing Marcia Johnson would get would probably have been one of Janie’s fingers. That wasn’t going to happen on my watch.’

‘Right, now listen to me and listen carefully, okay?’

‘I’m listening.’

‘I have made this missing girl an official enquiry. It’s been shifted over to my office, seeing that Organised Crime and Bogdan was involved.’

‘So you want me to pull out?’ No way would I do that.

‘No, no, I don’t want you to pull out. I said listen, so just listen.’

‘Okay.’ Yes sir.

‘Remember I told you I’d take an unofficial look at the Essex job, and I have. There were three AROs involved – their reports of the sting says the plane didn’t drop anything, but veered off at the last moment. The pilot must have seen something, probably them or their vehicles, and no money or drugs were found at the scene. Randall must have got a message from the pilot as he was out of the vehicle and started shooting wildly into the thicket – one of the AROs took a bullet to the arm and that’s when the others shot back and hit Randall. His driver sped off and got away.’

‘Nothing in the news reports of the time about a driver?’

‘No, there’s not.’

‘Is that where the money is?’

‘With the driver?’

‘Yes.’

‘No, there wouldn’t have been any money at the scene, why would there be? The pilot’s not going to open a window, put out his hand and collect it as he flies past, is he? Randall would have had the money from the buyer before the delivery and either sorted it away into an offshore account ready to send to the drug cartel after he received the package, or he'd sent it already. Most drug deals are delivery then payment.'

'Be nice to know who the driver was, he might know where the money is.'

'Yes.'

'What are you going to do next?

'Nothing until we get the girl back.'

'We?' I didn't like the '*we*' bit.

'I can get the Romanian police to work with you – they have a unit called the Special Operations Directorate who I've worked with before on getting info on Romanian organised crime gangs with branches over here.'

'No, definitely not – I do this solo. I don't want anybody to know I'm coming, least of all the local police. The Bogdan family is big, you know that – big and rich, and they would have friends in the force.'

'You worried about leaks?'

'Yes. You're the only person who knows what I'm doing, so if it goes belly-up and something happens to me Gold has orders to kill you.'

'I hope you are kidding, Nevis.'

'I am, but you and I are the only ones on this at the moment. Let's keep it that way until I get the girl back and trace the money.'

Clancy thought for a few moments. 'Okay, but if it does go belly-up you are on your own. I know nothing about it, and we've not had this conversation.'

'You'd better change your SIM card then.'

'I will.'

'One thing you can do.'

'Yes?'

'Harry Cohen, theatrical agent with offices in Wardour Street – he's a bit player in all this as far as I know, but he might be bigger than he lets on. Keep an eye on him, he might try to hop it. You can get his photo off the internet – might be worth putting a flag on him at the borders.'

'Harry Cohen… Okay, will do.'

'And another thing.'

'Yes?'

'Do you realise how much you've just cost the British taxpayer in mobile roaming charges?'

'Bollocks.'

Click.

I went back to my clouds with a slight smile on my face. I'd managed to keep official law enforcement out of the case, which meant I could make decisions and generally wreak havoc if I needed to. One thing was for sure, Janie Johnson was coming home with me.

CHAPTER 8

I changed five hundred pounds into euros at the money exchange in Debrecen Airport and used some of it to rent a Range Rover at the SIXT car rental counter, all cash and using my George Hadlow passport and international driver's licence. I always carry a thousand pounds in fifties in a small waterproof wallet strapped to my left ankle. I never use ATMs abroad; I wasn't going to leave a trace of the real me anywhere. The drive over the border to Romania was without incident, drove straight through.

I got a text from Gold, *Marriot Hotel name Mr and Mrs Springer.* Gold likes dogs. That didn't mean we'd be sharing a room – she would have booked another room for herself – but by booking a double for Mr and Mrs it meant that if anything went wrong and I had to take a low profile at the hotel, the police would be checking the hotels for a recent booking for a single male, not a couple.

I parked up in the hotel car park and checked in, keeping my head down and my face away from the CCTV camera. Fifth floor; nice room – should be for €180! Gold had paid upfront – cash, no doubt. So that was a bill going Marcia's way sometime in the future, together with the cost of the flights. I took a shower, changed into casual and sent a text to Gold to say I was in. I checked my watch: four o'clock. With a bit of luck I'd have Janie out from wherever the Bogdans were holding her that night and back to Debrecen, onto the charter flight and home by the morning. Well, that's the plan. Simple, eh? Well, aren't they all on paper.

Gold came into my room half an hour later. She was dressed to kill – and by that I mean literally to kill. All in black: black jeans, black ankle boots, black sweater and black padded jacket over a stab-proof vest. She had her Burberry shoulder bag with her; Gold's shoulder bag is our toolbox, inside would be night vision glasses, gloves, balaclavas, earpieces and clip mics with belt clip batteries, and double-edged eight-inch knives and sheaths, flares and a grenade. See what I mean? Dressed to kill. If she'd been stopped at Customs I'd probably be bailing her out now.

She took out a street map and laid it out on the table.

'She's here.' Gold pointed to a street not far from the hotel. 'It's a club called The Amsterdam, big place with three floors above. The club's in the basement, so Janie will be upstairs somewhere. First floor is illegal gaming with machines and tables, and then second and third are the Bogdans' storerooms and living space. If you get in and find her, the only way out without risking being seen is down a steel zigzag fire escape bolted on the back of the building that comes down into a back alley. And it is an alley, not wide enough for a car.'

I sat back. 'How do you know all this?'

'The wonderful internet – the city planner's office is all online, plans of just about every building in the city.' She pulled out a copy of a building plan. 'This is The Amsterdam Club – I looked it up, went back to the original planning permission details and hey presto.' She pushed it in front of me. 'All the planning details down to where the gambling machines and table were to be put and every room labelled, '*birouri*', office, '*magazine*', stores, and '*spatiu de locuit*', living area.'

'A burglar's route map, eh?'

'*Your* route map – study it.' She stood to go. 'I'm going to go and have a good look round, I'll be back about ten o'clock – be ready. Everything's in here.' She put the shoulder bag on the bed. 'If you eat, get room service to bring something up. Don't leave the room – we don't want your face on any CCTV.' And with that instruction she left without another word.

I ordered a chicken salad and coffee and watched the BBC World News on the TV as I ate it – nothing about the Bucharest Club in London – set my mobile alarm for nine and then slept.

****

The mobile buzzed and woke me up. It wasn't nine and caller ID showed Gold. I swung my legs off the bed and took it.

'Yes?'

'You've got company.'

'I'm listening.'

'I was checking the alley behind The Amsterdam Club and two heavies came out. I followed them in case the Bogdans had another place nearby where the girl might be. They came straight to the hotel, spent some time at reception, and are now outside your door. I'll do a walk by and we can do a double shift. I'll take your left-hand one'

'Okay.'

A double shift is an attack method using one of you from the front of the targets and one from the back. Gold taking the left hand one meant she'd take care of the one on my left when I opened the door; I had to take the one on the right.

'Five seconds.'

I moved to the side of the door. If I'd looked through the peephole I'd probably have seen another eye looking in, so I kept under it, counting the seconds away in my head – *one Mississippi, two Mississippi, three Mississippi, four Mississippi, five Mississippi...* I pulled the door open as fast as I could and reached for the coat lapels of the goon on the right, pulling him towards me into the room, and smashed my forehead into his nose before he knew what was happening. I swung him round, kicked him in the back of his legs so he went down on his knees, and putting a lock on his head twisted until the sudden relaxation of his body told me I'd broken his neck and he was dead. I let him slump to the floor and turned to help Gold. Needless to say, she didn't need any help; her goon was already dead, face down on the floor, blood seeping from the slit in his carotid neck artery onto a very expensive Marriot carpet. Gold kicked the room door shut behind her and went into the bathroom to clean blood from her knife and hands. I searched their overcoat pockets and found what I was looking for: each had a PPKS 9mm short pistol with a full clip.

I took the duvet from the bed and covered the bodies.

'That was lucky,' I said as she came back out, and I passed one of the pistols over and pocketed the other. Gold checked it over and put it in the shoulder bag.

'We have to be clear by the morning, room service comes round about ten,' she said, pushing the clean knife back into the sheaf Velcroed round her right ankle and switching on the hotel's electric kettle. 'Tea?' I think there must be an English ancestor somewhere in her family history.

Good job I'd persuaded Clancy not to involve the local police; we'd been in the country a few hours and already two dead! Let's hope they're not missed and nobody comes looking for them. Hotel reception would say they came up to this room.

We drank our tea and went over the plan of the club building again. If Janie was there she'd be on one of the upper floors, probably the one with the stores; if the top two floors were living quarters I couldn't see whoever lived there wanting a hostage for company. I wouldn't see how to get up from the ground floor until I was inside, although there was always the fire escape on the back. First problem was getting into the club. I had thought of creating another 'Big Tony' incident, but I'd prefer to get inside quietly and un-noticed as it might take time to find Janie. I would need a distraction to get me in, something Gold specialises in.

We finished our tea and I went into the bathroom and changed into my black gear: black suede ankle boots with thick rubber soles, black polo neck thermal jumper and black jeans with thigh, shin and back pockets, and of course my stab-proof vest. I put my knife sheath round my right ankle, the PKK in my right pocket, safety on, and fastened our communication battery pack onto my belt, pushed in my earpiece and clipped my microphone onto my polo neck; all wireless, so no leads to get tangled or pulled out. I was all set. Last thing was black gloves and balaclava ready for use in left thigh pocket. I gave Gold the hire car keys and told her whereabouts in the hotel garage it was; I always try to park as near to a car park exit as I can, for obvious reasons. Once I was in the club, Gold would fetch the car and be on hand for a speedy getaway, with or without Janie Johnson, but hopefully with her.

Gold took the lift to the main entrance and I took the overcoat from my goon, checked it wasn't bloody, slipped it on over my black gear and made my way out down the back stairs to the car park, onto the hotel front apron and across into the street. Darkness had thrown its cape over Bucharest. *Hello darkness, my old friend.*

CHAPTER 9

The Amsterdam Club was busy, very busy – I liked that, crowds give good cover. The queue of punters waiting to get in past the two very large doorman was a good fifty metres long and spilling from the pavement into the road. I edged near to the front of the queue on the opposite side of the road and waited for Gold to start the show.

I didn't have to wait long; a verbal altercation near the front of the queue quickly escalated to pushing and shoving as Gold pushed herself in. I watched the doormen taking a look and then exchanging words and laughter. That changed when a perfectly placed right uppercut from Gold laid out a young man on the pavement and all hell broke loose. The doormen were quick to skip down the club steps two at a time and push into the crowd. I was just as quick to skip up the steps, through the doors and into the club. Others in the queue had the same idea and quickly followed; that was good, the more the better. Any inside security hadn't a chance of stopping them and the many others who had the same idea behind them.

Inside the entrance to the club a short wide foyer area led to wide stairs going down to the dance area from where the incessant thud, thud, thud of dance beats could be heard. On the left before the stairs was a door marked *'numai personalul',* staff only. I tried it and it opened. Once inside I closed it behind me and took stock of my bearings. I was in a corridor lit by fluorescent strips, with doors on both sides. I worked quickly along; the first two were an empty office and a storeroom, and the third door opened into a cloakroom, presumably for staff clothes as there were club logo T-shirts on a table and coats on wall hangers. I took off my borrowed goon overcoat and hung it up, taking my balaclava from my pocket and putting it on with my night vision glasses fastened tight around my forehead, ready to be flicked down to my eyes if needed. I took the PPK from the overcoat and slipped it into my right-hand thigh pocket, then I continued my room search. Next was a room of boxes – no time to look inside – followed by a room of old promotional material, stand-up adverts for events and a toilet. At the end of the corridor another door opened onto stairs going up and down; I chose up. I remembered the plan, the next floor would be the Casino; there was nobody on the stairs, so presumably it was shut.I crept up and I was right; double glass doors showed the Casino empty, lights off.

Onto the next floor which should be more promising; this would be the storerooms on the building plan. A swing door led off the stairs into a corridor; a pair of lift doors on the left seemed to fit the storerooms scenario – crates of beer were heavy to carry up and down stairs, so the lift must be for getting that. The LED indicator showed the lift to be on the bottom floor; must be the actual club room. I checked the rooms along the corridor; yes, all stores, with beer barrels, crates and boxes of bottled spirits and bar snacks.

A noise from the lift shaft caught my attention. The LED was now one above the bottom; the lift was on its way up, and this floor was next. I slipped quickly into the first room and stood to the side of the closed door. Anyone opening it wouldn't see me until they stepped right into the room, by which time they'd be out cold. I hoped the lift would carry on up to the living accommodation floors. It didn't.

I heard a metallic scraping as the lift doors opened and then voices; two people, both male. They gave my door a miss and went into the next room. I heard crates being pulled from that room along the corridor and into the lift – quite a few, business in the club must be good. At last the lift doors clanged shut and it was gone. I peeked out of the room; all clear, the lift LED showed at the bottom again. I carried on with the rooms. The last one was locked – none of the others had been locked. I hadn't time to play around with lock picks – anyway, I hadn't got a pair with me

– and it looked a common or garden cheap Yale one lever cylinder lock that wouldn't offer much resistance, I planted my right boot dead centre on the lock with as much force as I could give. There was a loud splintering of wood and the door swung open, taking half the jamb with it. I moved quickly inside and knelt in the darkness, my gun poised in my right hand as my left flicked down my night vision glasses.

It was a big room, bigger than the others, with the back half-partitioned off halfway to the ceiling with a door-sized opening. Something moved with a slight noise behind the partition. I moved quickly to the wall and crept silently along until I reached the partition, and laying sideways on the floor slid towards the opening; if there was anybody inside they wouldn't expect me to be lowdown, and if armed would be aiming chest-high towards the opening. Slowly I looked around the opening; in the darkness my night visions picked out a figure huddled on the floor in the far corner.

'Janie?' I whispered across the floor.

'Yes,' came back a trembling answer.

'Is there anybody in there with you?'

'No.'

I stood and walked in, checking around just in case. She was alone. There was a light switch by the opening; I flicked it and a single bulb hanging from the ceiling lit up the partitioned area. Janie

Johnson was sat in a far corner on a mattress, next to a small table on which the remains of a bowl of soup and a bottle of mineral water stood. She stood up; she was wearing a blue boiler suit and I noticed her left wrist had a wide steel bracelet fastened round it like a handcuff, with a chain going from it to a hasp set into the floor. That was going to be a problem.

'Who are you?' Her voice was still trembling.

'Mummy sent me. Don't ask questions just do as I say, okay? Questions can come later.'

She nodded. 'Okay.'

I pointed to the bracelet. 'Where's the key?'

'They have it, they unlock it when I go to the toilet.'

'When's that, once a day?'

'No, no, I call and somebody comes.' She pointed to a cheap child's battery intercom on the table.

'Call now.'

'Now?'

'Yes, now.'

I walked out of the partition area and out of the room as she pressed it. I took a gamble that whoever answered Janie's call of nature would come from the door at the end of the corridor, which I guessed would lead to a staircase like the other end of the corridor had. I went into the room nearest that end and waited. I had to get to whoever came before they saw the damage to the door to Janie's room and raised the alarm. I had to be quick. I stood behind the door, keeping it open just a crack so I could see who went past; hopefully it would be just one person. It was, one middle-aged lady wearing an apron – staff from the living quarters upstairs? I quietly slipped out behind her and brought the gun down hard and fast on the side of her head with my right hand, as my left arm encircled her as she slumped forward. I pulled her through the broken door and into where Janie waited. Her eyes opened wide in horror.

'Don't worry, she's not dead.' I lowered the lady onto the mattress, pulled the key to the bracelet from the apron pocket and took it off Janie's wrist. I could see her wrist was red raw with the chafing. Nice people, the Bogdans – they could have put a bandage on first. I slipped the bracelet onto the lady's wrist, clicked it shut and threw the key into the opposite corner.

'Right, let's go. Stay close.'

'Hang on.' Janie gave the woman a good hard kick in the ribs, which brought a moan from her lips.

I raised my eyebrows at Janie.

'It's what she did to me every time,' she explained, and gave the body one for luck. 'Bastard bitch.'

I was beginning to like Janie, a lot.

We left the room and went along to the end of the corridor and through the door onto the stairs. I thought about calling the lift, but I didn't know where it ended up on the ground floor, and really didn't like the prospect of the doors opening in front of a load of Bogdan's goons. I started up the stairs; I reasoned that there would be an exit onto the outside fire escape from the next floor, as that was marked as the living accommodation on the plan. Two zigzag flights of stairs up and we came to a small landing and a wall with a door. Music and voices were coming from inside. Too dangerous; if it was a living area there would be people, and people around Bogdan have guns. One or two I could deal with, but maybe there would be kids as well. Complicated. If we got trapped on that floor by goons coming up the stairs, we'd be in deep trouble.

I shook my head at Janie and started back down; she didn't argue, just followed. I was hoping that somewhere off the stairs there might be a door leading out to the fire escape bolted onto the outside of the building, but there wasn't. At the bottom of the stairs we could feel the thud of the disco music through the floor as we made our way along a corridor. Halfway along a door on the right was open and a flashing strobe light permeated through. We must be behind the club's bar; beside the door on the floor were three crates of beer bottles which must have been the ones I'd seen loaded into the lift upstairs earlier. The lift was on the opposite side of the corridor, doors closed. We made our way slowly along. In front of us a man suddenly stepped out from the open door and bent to drag a crate back through it. Lucky for him he bent away from us and didn't see us. My gun was aimed towards him all the while as Janie and I stood stock still, willing him not to turn our way. He did the same for the other two crates before the door slammed shut behind him.

I smiled at Janie. 'Phew.'

She didn't reply. We hurried past the door to the end of the corridor which had a heavy steel door set into it, the type that emergency exits have with a bar across that you push down to open. I pushed and it opened. We went quickly inside and I closed it behind us. The light was a dim red bulb hanging from the ceiling; there were no other doors. A closed room? We were trapped. The only way out was to retrace our steps past the bar. I noticed two large bolts on the door – why would you want to bolt yourself inside this room? I was about to tell Janie that we had to go back when she tugged my arm and pointed to the corner of the room.

'Look.'

I looked. A metre-square trapdoor was set into the concrete floor. Perhaps there was a cellar beneath? I took a closer look; it had a hasp and staple latch locked by a combination set padlock.

'Go into the corner and get down facing the wall, with your hands over your ears,' I told Janie, pointing towards the far corner.

She hurried across and did just that. I shot the padlock off. No silencer on the goon's gun, so the bang reverberated around the room. Surely they must have heard that in the bar? Quickly I pushed the door bolts across; they were a sturdy kind and would hold fast against anybody trying to open the door from the outside. I kicked the padlock remains off the hasp and pulled up the trapdoor. Inside it looked like a pitch black hole, with an iron stairway fastened on the side disappearing down into the darkness. There was a switch set into the side, so I reached in and flicked it. Twelve feet below a shaft of light lit the bottom of the hole; it led down to a tunnel entrance at the bottom. Only one thing to do then: use it.

'Down you go.'

This girl was good – no if and buts, she was down that ladder as fast as she could go. I followed and pulled the trapdoor shut above me. It had two good strong gate bolts, their receiving holes drilled into the concrete side of the shaft. I slid them home.

With them and the bolts on the room door, this was obviously an escape route for the Bogdans if the law came calling in force.

I stepped off the bottom rung and stood beside Janie, looking along the tunnel. It was a very professional job: three metres-high by two wide, with fluorescent tubes lighting it every ten metres. I half-expected to see a motorbike with stabilizers parked ready to go like the Chapo Guzman prison escape tunnel. No such luck, we had to walk. I started off; were I on my own I would be racing along, but I had to take into account she'd been locked up with no exercise for a while, so the muscles would be complaining by now. I rolled up my balaclava into a beanie hat.

'You okay?' I asked over my shoulder.

'Can we rest?'

'No.' I slowed down. 'Once they find you gone and realise we took the tunnel, they'll get to wherever it comes out and be waiting – so we need to get there before them.'

'Okay.'

'I have to make a call, so take a quick break.'

'A call?'

I lifted my sweater to show Janie the com,s battery and switched it on. We wouldn't be too far below ground to block a signal.

'Nevis to Gold.'

'Where the fuck have you been? I've been calling for ages!' Gold was angry. Gold doesn't swear.

'I've got Janie with me – we are in an escape tunnel leading from the club, don't know where it leads. Will let you know as soon as I do.'

'Okay, I'm in the car. Keep the line open. There's not a lot of activity at the club, so perhaps they haven't noticed she's gone yet.'

'Hope so.'

I turned to Janie who couldn't hear Gold's side of the conversation coming through my earpiece. 'My partner thinks they haven't sussed that you've gone yet. We need to keep going to keep ahead of them. Come on.'

I set off again and Janie followed with renewed effort; good news can have a lifting effect.

I estimated we'd gone about three hundred metres when the tunnel ended with another steel door. Large bolts held it firm, but luckily no padlocks; whoever built this tunnel wanted to exit fast, as they were well greased. I slid the bolts across and slowly pulled the door; it opened inwards, which I thought was unusual. As I opened it the light from our tunnel showed another tunnel, a much bigger one forming a T junction with ours going off left and right. It was pitch black. I was about to step out when a Bucharest

Metro train hurtled past, causing such an air rush into our tunnel that it flattened the pair of us onto our backs.

I hadn't seen the rail track from our tunnel as the exit was set in the wall well above it; we had a good five foot drop down to the maintenance walkway that skirted beside it. I leaned carefully and slowly out, looking both ways and listening. Silence. To the left I could see the platform lights of a station about sixty metres away, the train that had sped by was standing at the platform filling with late night revellers on their way home. It blocked out most of the view and would act as a shield stopping people seeing us from the platform as the rear of the last carriage was just poking into the tunnel.

'Come on.' I jumped down to the walkway and reached up to help Janie down. We kept stooped down as we hurried towards the rear of the train; there was a platform step up to a door into the rear of the last carriage, and I took it and looked inside through the window. It was a guard's compartment, no guard; the door from it into the rear carriage proper was shut, with a blind down over the glass. I opened the door and stepped inside, turning to haul Janie up from the line as the train began to move off; she stepped inside and I closed the door as she sank to the floor exhausted. I looked out of the side window; the station was Izvor – didn't mean a thing to me, but looking back down the fast disappearing empty platform four men had appeared down the stairs from the street above and were congregated at the entrance to the main tunnel we'd come out of. Janie's absence had been noted. We'd made it, but only just.

'Shit!'

'What?' There was a note of fear in Janie's voice.

'They know you're out.'

I clicked my mic on.

'Gold?'

'I'm listening.'

I knew she would be. 'We are on a metro train.' I looked up at the metro map stuck on the wall. 'Just left Izvor station, the next on the map is Timpuri Noi. Can you meet us there?'

'Hang on, I'll take a look on my mobile.'

There was a ten second pause.

'Yes, got it, I'm not far. I'll pull up as near as I can opposite the station entrance – traffic's busy so wait if I'm not there before you.'

'Okay, and by the way, they know Janie's gone so take care.'

'Will do.'

Click.

Janie looked up at me from the floor. 'Are you going to tell me what all this is about now?'

'No, not now – we have other things to concentrate on. At the next station my partner will be meeting us there with a car. When the train pulls into the station, we separate and get in amongst the crowd and make our way up to the street. I'll be behind you, but don't look round – merge in. When you get to the street, cross it and wait there – get in a shop doorway if you can, and wait. She's in a black Range Rover, one lady driver all in black. Understand?'

She nodded. 'Yes.'

We were already slowing down as the train pulled into Timpuri Noi. It was thankfully a busy station. I waited until half those leaving the train were off and those getting on were squeezing past into the carriages, and then opened the guard door and we left. I followed Janie along the platform, dodging between the people and then off it onto the *up* escalator. I stayed a good ten metres behind; I had it in my mind that the goons at Izvor station would see the tunnel door from their club to the line was open and guess we must have taken a train. Then it was guesswork; would we stay on board to the end of the line, or get off before that? They wouldn't have enough immediate manpower to send people to all the stations, and in any case we might change lines at one, so I took a guess they'd be on their way to Timpuri Noi. I just hoped we'd get out before they arrived.

We didn't; Janie did. We got across the station entrance hall and into the street amongst the crowds; she darted through the bumper-to-bumper traffic to the far side of the road and into a dark shop doorway, well-hidden by passing pedestrians. I stayed the station side of the road watching for Bogdan's men and Gold. I hoped she would arrive first and we could be on our way. She didn't; they did. I saw them leave a large BMW CRV that pulled into the kerb and stopped fifty metres up the road, which was as close as it could get to a parking space. Four goons – no disguising what they were – got out and jostled and bumped people out of their way as they made towards the station. I stood back out of sight against a side wall of the station foyer and knelt down, appearing to fiddle with my right bootlaces as I slipped my knife out of its ankle sheath.

The first two passed me hurrying into the station hall; the other two stood on the kerb looking around. I slipped into the crowd leaving the hall again and onto the street, edging over towards the goons who were more concerned with checking the travellers coming off the escalator than those in the street. When I was near enough I stepped quickly between them from behind and stabbed both their thighs, quickly and with force. They sank to the pavement screaming in pain as I bent low and ran away through the traffic and across the road. The crowd panicked and started running in all directions, which suited me. I nodded to Janie to follow me and we merged into the fleeing horde along the pavement away from the scene.

Gold came on the comms. *'What's happening, there's a riot or something at the station?'*

'Two down, but there's another two at the station. Drive past, we are further along the road.'

I pulled Janie into a doorway and looked back towards the station; the traffic was moving past us slowly, with drivers trying to rubberneck what was happening, horns blaring at the people running between the cars, and in the distance sirens began wailing. I knelt and slipped my knife back into its sheath and spied Gold in the Range Rover ten cars back, making her way slowly towards us. I pulled Janie into a shop doorway.

'See the black Range Rover about ten cars back?'

'Yes.'

'That's ours. When it gets level, walk out slowly and get in the back.'

'Okay.'

She did exactly that. Gold nodded to me from the driver's seat. I clicked on my comms. 'I'm going to ride shotgun for a while.'

'Okay.'

The car moved away in the slow traffic, I backed into the shop doorway and waited, watching the road back to the station. It wasn't long before I saw what I was expecting. The other two goons plus two more were hurrying along the road, two either side of the traffic queue checking the cars for us. They probably would know what Janie looks like, but they wouldn't know me so surprise was on my side. I checked on Gold's progress; traffic was still slow but she was a good hundred metres away up the road.

Turning away from the crowd I pulled out the gun and slipped the safety off before holding it in my pocket. The goons were too intent on checking the cars than to worry about people on the pavement or in the road; an ideal assassin scenario, I would have the jump on them. That felt good. Why do I always feel good when I am about to hurt somebody? Gotta get counselling someday.

I let them pass me by checking cars further up the line and then I slowly stepped back into the pavement crowd and moved along until I was nearly level with them. My first two bullets were easy; I was right behind goon number one and he probably felt the steel barrel against the back of his head before the bullet went through it. Goon number two hardly had time to register what was happening as he turned around before bullet number two buried itself in his heart. I still had the advantage, as goons three and four's tiny brains had to work out whether it was their partners shooting at somebody or somebody shooting at their partners. Before they could work that out, I moved in a stoop round the back of the car they were looking at and took them out; goon three fell to the ground with the hole in his neck pumping blood onto the road, and goon four slumped over the car bonnet, his body twitching. I stepped forward and finished him with one to the back of the head which went right through, and then through the bonnet and lodged somewhere in the car's engine. I shrugged an apology at the terrified driver and passenger before quickly running off. The crowd nearest to the incident were not sure what to do; some stood aghast, others fled. Those fleeing would be looking where they were going and wouldn't realise I was the shooter as I sped past most of them.

Gold was a good two hundred yards up the road where the traffic had cleared and was parked at the kerb. I slipped into the passenger seat. She raised her eyebrows.

'All clear?'

'All clear.'

'Debrecan then?

'Yes.' I could see she had already got the route to the airport up on the dashboard satnav. I looked at the inside mirror and could see Janie sitting quietly in the back. I spoke to Gold loud enough for

Janie to hear. 'I think there's a young lady in the back who might have a lot of questions.'

Gold nodded. 'Okay, but let's get out of the city unscathed first. The Bogdans won't be very happy people now and they will be throwing everything at finding us. Explanations can come later.' As usual Gold had the priorities in the right order. Yes ma'am.

I turned to Janie. 'You okay with that?'

She nodded and said with a smile, 'I'm beginning to think I might have strayed onto the set of a James Bond film.'

I returned the smile. 'Well let's hope it doesn't turn into a Johnny English one, eh?'

We all smiled. I busied myself putting a new magazine into the gun – six bullets is better than two. I got on the mobile to the charter plane pilot and told him to register a flight plan with Debrecan Tower for the UK and be ready to take off at ten minutes' notice. Marcia Johnson was going to have a heavy bill to pay, but what's money compared to a daughter's life?

We cleared the city limits without any trouble, nobody was following us – well, nobody we could see. Time to update Janie. I took her from the first meeting I had with Harry Cohen and her mum up to getting into The Amsterdam Club and finding her. I left out most of the killings.

'The rest you know.' I relaxed, wondering what was going through her mind. It was Harry Cohen.

'I never trusted Harry Cohen. I told mum time and time again to get another agent – he's lightweight, no clout in the business. Her best work comes direct from people in the business who know her, know how good she is – always has. Cohen is all commercials and soap operas. She won't leave him, she's too loyal. The only time he takes his finger out and gets her work is when I have a go at him and threaten to take her and myself elsewhere. She's not got a contract with him, you know – I wouldn't let her sign one, no way.'

The big surprise was Janie didn't mention her father.

'You haven't said anything about your father, James Randall, so I assume you knew about him all along?'

She gave an audible smirk. 'Him, yes – another of Harry Cohen's little surprises. I never worried at all about who my father was, he never was in my life and I had no thoughts or wishes of being in his, whoever he was. Mum and I were good together – I introduced her to many suitors.' She laughed. 'Imagine that, the single daughter introducing her mum to suitable men. Anyway, Harry called me into his office one day and acted like some benevolent older relative and introduced me to James Randall, and dropped the bomb that he was my father. Knowing Harry, I knew there must be an angle in it for him. I didn't think it would lead to all this though. I was quite rude, told him and Randall that I and mum had absolutely no need of either of them, and for Harry to foist that on me was about as low as he could get, and I stormed out.'

'Did you tell your mum?'

'No, as far as I was concerned that was the end of that. Harry was round to my flat later that day and apologising – said he had made a terrible mistake and I wouldn't hear from Randall again. And I didn't. I looked him up on Google and press cuttings – I have a press cutting agency that monitors all the newspapers and social media for anything about me, most actors have – so I asked them to delve into James Randall. Told them I was up for a part in a true crime series that involved him.'

'I bet you got a surprise.'

'Didn't I just! God, no wonder mum ditched him – why she ever got involved with him in the beginning I just don't know.'

'Well, the bottom line is that the Bogdans think she is *still* involved with him, or was up until his death, and they think your mum has their money.'

'Which is why I am sitting in the back of a car in Romania.'

‘Yes. With ten intact fingers.’

‘What?’

‘That would have been next if we hadn’t got you out – another note to your mum for the money, neatly wrapped around one of your fingers.’

Gold added, ‘Or ear.’

Janie was visibly shocked. ‘What do we do?’

‘You do nothing –when we get back you disappear with mum, go to a hotel somewhere far away whilst I find where the money went. I’ve got some leads.’

Gold gave me a sideways glance that said, *‘Really?’* I didn’t respond. I wanted to know one more thing. ‘What happened on the day you were kidnapped?’

‘Window cleaners.’

‘Window cleaners? They came in through your windows?’

She gave a small laugh. ‘No, the landlord has a contract with a cleaning company to clean the outside of the windows. There was a buzz on the intercom and the man said he was from a company taking over the contract for the landlord, and could he come and take a look from the inside. I had no reason not to let him, and when I opened the door there were two of them. One gave me their flyer, and when I let them in and shut the door, that was it. I was bundled into the lounge, made to drink a small glass of water from the kitchen, and that's all I remember.'

Gold exchanged a glance with me. 'Rohypnol.'

I nodded agreement.

'What?' Janie asked.

'They probably gave you the drug Rohypnol,' I told her. 'Known as the date-rape drug – knocks you out. How long were you unconscious?'

'I don't know. I woke up in the back of a big lorry, bound and gagged with sacks of animal feed all around me. I hadn't been raped. It seemed hours I was in it, then I was taken out at the building where you found me and chained in that room.'

****

We travelled on, keeping a look out behind us, but the other traffic seemed normal; none moving up close with a gun held pointing our way from the passenger window. Well, that's how they do it in the movies, so it must be true.

'That's not right.' Gold slowed down and slipped into a short layby at the side of the road. Ahead of us the Romanian-Hungarian border post had a queue of cars waiting to go through. It shouldn't have. Hungary and Romania are part of the European Union Shengen agreement, a pact between all twenty-six European countries to officially abolish passport control and all other types of border control at their mutual borders. The traffic should be driving straight through; it wasn't. Each car was being stopped and searched.

'Stay here until you hear from me,' I said to Gold as I got out of the car and put my night visions on and switched on my comms.

'Okay.' Gold reached for her comms battery pack and switched on too.

I waited until no cars were coming and then jumped the low fence into the farmer's field that ran alongside the road. It was pasture, not a ploughed field, which made running through it quite easy. I moved a good fifty metres into the field where passing headlights wouldn't pick me out and went towards the non-existent border, which seemed to be a hedgerow leading alongside the field down to the border post. I turned and keeping down made it quickly to the back of the concrete border post building. Gold had been right; something here was wrong. The cars leaving Romania were being stopped and searched by civilians, not uniformed border guards.

I took out my gun, slipped the safety catch off and moved around the dark side of the building away from the queuing cars and their lights. Through the side window I could see two Border Control guards tied and gagged on the floor, with a civilian with a gun standing in the front doorway watching, as another three searched the cars one by one before letting them pass through; all carried guns. Bogdan's goons had taken over the post; how the Hell had they got here so quickly. I scoured the area through the night visions and there it was: a four-seater helicopter sitting in the dark fifty metres into the next field. I moved over to it and using a handy rock smashed all the dials and switches, before making my way back to the side of the post. I called Gold.

'Okay, join the queue. There's four of Bogdan's men, they've taken over the post. Put Janie in the passenger seat and when you get here take out the one who comes to your side of the car – I'll take the other three.'

'Okay.'

I moved back into the darkness and waited; I could see the Range Rover in the queue twenty cars back. It didn't take long for it to be three cars back as the goons were looking for a man and a woman; their search was a quick look at who was in each vehicle and the inside of the boot if the car had one. I waited by the corner of the building in the dark, and as Gold drew up to the goon standing in front of her and holding his hand up to stop the car, I moved fast. Their attention was on the car; the one standing in the building doorway took my first bullet in the side of his head and crumpled to the floor. I heard Gold's shot take out the goon on her side of the car before the other two realised what was happening and didn't know which way to look; I took out the one standing at the front of the car with two body shots, and the one on the passenger side hadn't time to turn my way before the bullet in the back of the head from such a short distance pushed him forward to slump over the car roof and slide slowly down past Janie's look of horror as his bleeding head left blood smears down the passenger window beside her.

I jumped into the back and Gold floored the accelerator; we bumped over the body of the goon in front and were away. We had a few minutes before the people in the cars behind would be able to gather their thoughts and get out, and then a few minutes more before the guards were released and able to call their base. They hadn't seen us, so any description of the car was going to be amateur; and anyway, there's plenty of Range Rovers in Hungary and we'd be in Debrecen and at the airport before anything organised could happen.

Janie was quiet. I leant forward and put my hand on her shoulder. 'You okay?'

She half turned. 'You just killed four people.' Her voice shook.

'I wasn't counting.'

I could see a smile on Gold's face in the mirror.

'They might have families.'

Oh no, not that old chestnut again. I sat back. 'Yes, they probably do –and probably the people they killed in the past had families too.'

'Are there many people like you, Ben Nevis?'

'Not many, but you're lucky – mum hired the best.'

'You're a killer with no conscience.' It was said quietly and without any malice, but she'd nailed me perfectly.

'And you're a young lady with all her fingers and two ears.'

Gold stepped in. 'Don't worry, Janie. It doesn't happen a lot, but sometimes the world isn't a nice place, and things have to be put right.'

Janie mirror-traced a blood smear on the outside of the passenger window with her finger. 'I thought this kind of thing was just in films and Netflix.'

So do a lot of people, Janie, I thought to myself, so do a lot of people.

****

Everything at the airport was going smoothly, the pilot had done his job and the papers were all in order; nobody questioned that one person came in on the flight and three were going out on it. That's the beauty of charter flights; officials have enough paperwork to navigate their way through with the regular timetable passenger flights, yet alone adding any for a light charter flight, especially at two in the morning. Mind you, the company I use are good; they register flights as 'freight', so immigration take no notice of them. Crafty, eh? It was as we taxied to the end of the runway that things hotted up.

The pilot turned to me. 'The tower want us to return to the parking area.'

I shook my head. 'No way, we go.'

'Okay.'

The pilot didn't reply to the tower and put the intercom on speaker.

'One seven four five two, return to your stand.'

'One seven four five two to control, you're breaking up – please repeat?'

'One seven four five two, abort your take off – repeat, abort your take off.'

'One seven four five two, your message is unclear – lots of static on the line. Please repeat.'

By now we were on the departure runway and gathering speed. The pilot shut off the speaker and waved a thumb over his shoulder pointing behind us. I looked back and two cars with blues flashing were on the tarmac and gaining on us.

'Friends come to see you off?' The pilot was a sarcastic so-and-so when he wanted to be. I'd used him before, and he knew I wasn't always strictly legit.

'Definitely not.'

'Okay.' He pulled a switch on the controls and a valve on each of the kerosene tanks on the wings opened, spilling the fuel out onto the runway behind us. 'That should do it,' he said after a few seconds and shut the valves.

Behind us the cars hit the fuel spill and danced together like two drunks on ice, spinning into each other and sliding across the runway out of control.

Then we were airborne and heading home.

Janie spent the flight back in silence. I thought it best to leave her alone with her thoughts. At Stansted Dick Clancy met us, introduced himself, put Janie in an unmarked police car with a couple of plain-clothed protection officers and sent her to Marcia's house with strict instructions to talk to no one. I thought about going with her, but maybe best to let mum and daughter sort themselves out on their own in the peace of the family home. I knew there would be officers inside and outside the house, so I didn't have any worries about their safety.

Darkness was turning into morning daybreak. I invited Gold back to mine for breakfast, but like me she wanted to just relax and unwind so we went our separate ways. I said I'd call later that day, so home to a long hot bath and bed.

CHAPTER 10

Harry Cohen was slumped forward over his desk. The exit wound of the bullet that had killed him showed large and jagged in the back of his head.

'The brothers are getting impatient.' Clancy stood with me beside the desk watching SOCOs in their paper suits going about their forensic business around the body and the office. A pathway of PCR plates led from the door to the desk; we made our way back across them and stepped off into the outer office, where a distraught secretary was sitting with a WPC giving a statement. We ignored each other; not the time for any ribald banter.

I'd managed just four hours sleep when Clancy had rung me at ten that morning. Cohen's secretary had arrived for work and found him like this. The local force had gone in and secured the building, and when Cohen's name was checked on the computer it had flagged up that the Organised Crime Unit had an interest in him and Clancy was alerted. We both got there about the same time. He hadn't mentioned anything about Romania yet.

'You didn't say much about your Romanian trip when you landed last night. All go to plan, did it?' He raised his eyebrows at me.

'Yes, pretty well – in and out. We weren't expected.'

'You didn't upset the Bogdan family so much that this is the result then?' He nodded towards Cohen.

'Well, they'd be upset that they'd lost their bargaining chip with Janie gone.'

Clancy nodded in agreement. 'And they obviously thought Cohen had something to do with it and wasn't of any further use to them.'

The pathologist wandered over. 'Pretty basic hit, single 9mm shot to the temple.'

'Well, at least he didn't suffer long,' said Clancy.

'He may have – he was tortured by the look of it.'

'Really?'

The pathologist referred to his notes. 'Burn marks on his forehead – looks like somebody stubbed out a cigarette on him.'

There are some nasty people around.

****

I rang Gold and arranged to meet her at the concourse cafe on Charing Cross Station. We use it a lot when a job's in operation, you can take a window seat and see everybody approaching; you can't do that in my office, and I thought it wise to give the office a wide berth as Cohen would have told his killers all about me, no doubt. If they didn't know I was involved before, they damn well would now, and there were still four Bogdan brothers to worry about. Although with a bit of luck a couple of them were amongst the bodies we'd left in Romania.

'You're not supposed to do that,' I admonished Gold as she poured herself a coffee from a thermos. 'You're supposed to buy it here.'

'If I make it myself, I know it's coffee and not dishwater. I don't know how you can drink that.' She nodded towards my cup of British Rail dishwater. She took a sip of her coffee. 'Lovely. Right, what happened at Cohen's then?'

'Well, I think we stirred up the family so much yesterday that they decided to attack hard. I don't know why they killed Cohen, he wouldn't offer any threat – I'd have thought they'd have gone to Marcia's house. Pretty obvious that's where Janie would be.'

'Or her flat.'

I hadn't thought of that – obvious, eh? 'Of course, her flat – Cohen would have given them her address. I bet there's a welcoming party waiting there.'

'Wanna check it out?'

'Later, leave them there for a few hours so they get bored and drop their guard. No rush.'

'Okay.' Gold cleared some space on the table. 'In the meantime I've been busy online this morning and calling in favours. Some interesting stuff.' She pulled a folder from her shoulder bag and put a paper from it in front of me. 'Harry Cohen's phone calls for the last two weeks – lots to Marcia and quite a few to Club Bucharest, and four to Romania.'

'Interesting – seems Harry was playing both sides.'

'His bank statement is even more interesting.' She flipped another paper in front of me. 'In the last six months Harry Cohen's little agency has moved three million through its account – bank transfers from Romania have come in regularly and gone out again pretty quickly to Belgium and Mexico.'

'Narco capitals.'

'Yes.'

I was getting the picture. 'So Randall was using Cohen's legitimate UK business account to get in the Bogdans' money for drug deals, then sending it by bank transfer to his suppliers in Mexico and Belgium to pay them once delivery was made.'

'Yes, and the timelines match – each amount coming in goes out about three weeks later with a shortfall of twelve percent, exactly twelve percent each time.'

It was all making sense. 'The three weeks being the time it takes for the drugs to be delivered, and the twelve percent skim being Randall's commission.'

Gold nodded. 'I'd agree with that – and then the twelve percent goes to an offshore account of a business registered in the Isle of Man.'

'Tax rate ten percent maximum.'

'Correct, so Randall's twelve percent of the three million transferred over the period is three hundred and sixty thousand pounds, of which he loses just thirty-six thousand in Manx tax, and everything is laundered and legal.'

'And no bundles of cash changing hands and splashing around being washed.'

'No, just a few clicks of the laptop keyboard. But there's an open ending which ties nicely in with what's going on. The last amount of a million in Cohen's account didn't go out to Mexico or Belgium, it went straight to the Isle of Man account.'

'Have you got the dates it came in and went out?'

'Of course. I'm ahead of you, Ben.' She smiled. 'The money came in to Harry Cohen's account from Romania before Randall was killed, and went out to the Isle of Man a good seven weeks afterwards.'

'This is all making sense. The Bogdans paid in advance for a consignment – the consignment that was supposed to be dropped from a small plane in Epping Forest – but when that went wrong and Randall was killed they didn't get their drugs, and somebody took the opportunity a few weeks later to transfer all the money into the Isle of Man account.'

'And obviously it wasn't Randall – he was dead.'

I agreed. 'No, and it wasn't Harry Cohen either – with a gun pointing to his head he would have folded and given the money back. He was killed because he was no further use to the Bogdans and knew too much about how they and Randall got the drugs into Romania. So whose account is it in the Isle of Man?'

Gold shrugged. 'Don't know, can't get any details. Offshore tax haven banks have the strongest security available – even your mate Clancy won't get anything from them, they sit outside UK legal jurisdiction. If they don't want to give you the information, they aren't obliged to.'

'If Harry Cohen knew whose account it was, he would have told the Bogdan brothers – and like you said, once they realised he didn't know, he was of no further use to them. Bang bang, goodbye

Harry. So who is this account holder, the mysterious third person? Is it the same person who was with Randall on the night he was killed in Epping Forest? What are we missing here?'

Gold laughed. 'That's exactly what we are missing – the name of the third person. Randall's partner, that's what we are missing.'

I took a sip of my coffee. It was stone cold; a bit like any leads to the missing person. I grimaced. 'Urgh.'

Gold held her thermos towards me. 'Top up? It's hot.'

'No, I'm fine. If we don't get any leads at Janie's tonight, I'll go and see Marcia Johnson tomorrow and get her to rack her brains and see if we can come up with any names Randall was close to. Let's hope she has a good memory.'

Gold checked her watch. I don't know why; habit I suppose, because there's a BR clock the size of Big Ben hanging from the concourse roof about fifty metres in front of the cafe.

'Gotta go.' She stood, put the folder back into her shoulder bag and slung it over her shoulder.

'Business?' I knew it would be.

'Yes.'

'Who's the lucky gent about to part with a small fortune?'

'Confidential information,' she tapped the side of her nose. 'But if he doesn't come up with my *very* reasonable demands, his colleagues in the House of Lords will be amazed by the pictures in the Sunday tabloids and on social media.' She smiled. 'And so will his wife. What time tonight?'

'Late, I think. If there's a welcome home party waiting at Janie's flat they'll be tired and fed up after sitting there all day. Meet you in the car park at eleven.'

'Which car park?'

I rented two car parking spaces at both my office and my apartment block; one for me and one for Gold.

'Home.'

'Okay.'

And she was gone. I must be the only private detective with a gold-digging blackmailer for a partner. Each to their own.

CHAPTER 11

We got to Janie's about eleven fifteen. The night had thrown its dark canopy over London and thankfully Janie's street wasn't well lit. None are these days; council funding cuts.

We were both in our black gear. I had my trusted Beretta 9mm in my pocket with a silencer fitted; made it a bit cumbersome, but a 9mm shot without a silencer would wake the whole of Fulham.

Gold drove her dark Lexus slowly along the street as we checked the inside of the parked cars; they all looked empty. She turned round at the end of the road and we came back and took another pass through, just in case we'd missed something. We had; a white van, no driver or passenger but a sign written on the sides and back: 'West London Cleaning Co.'

'Interesting,' I said, and pointed it out to Gold.

'Yes, very.' She took a left turn at the end of the road, made a three point turn and came back into Janie's street, pulling in and parking about sixty metres behind the rear of the van. She reached behind to the back seat and passed me the Nocoex night vision binoculars from her shoulder bag laying there. I flicked on the night vision mode and focused on the back of the van. These binoculars are like a small box with a LED screen at the rear; no holding them to the eyes, the screen shows what you are looking at. The van showed up with a green hue around it; no bright spots showing a heat source. That van must have been there for some time, or the tyres and exhaust would show up brighter than the rest. It was cold.

I passed the box to Gold. 'That's been there a long time.'

She agreed. 'Trouble is, we don't know if anybody's in the back.'

She was right. Body heat would only show up when looking directly at the body, not through the metal van. I switched to normal mode and took another look. The rear windows were blacked out. Nothing happening, or was there? I focused on the side of the van; light puffs of smoke were coming out of the passenger side window. I smiled, *gotcha*. Somebody inside was a smoker. The passenger window had been left open at the top for the smoke to escape! I passed the box to Gold. 'Passenger side window.'

She looked and a smile crossed her face as another puff of smoke left the gap. 'Filthy habit.'

'Smoking can kill you,' I said. 'Let's go.'

We left the Lexus; Gold crossed to the other side of the street while I stayed on the van's side and we walked in parallel towards it. No balaclavas this time; didn't want to scare the life out of any Fulham resident walking their dog. I sauntered past the rear of the van, looking as normal as I could in case somebody inside was watching through the back windows. They probably weren't, as Janie's house was to the front of where it was parked, so they'd be looking that way. I stopped alongside and peered across to Gold, who was stopped opposite. I pulled out the Beretta, slipped the safety off and gave Gold a nod; she moved across the road to the offside of the van.

We moved to the back, out of sight of the blacked-out windows. I gave another nod and Gold took my cue, and reaching across pulled the rear door open in a flash and held it wide. I stepped out to the opening and shot both the men sitting inside before they could realise what was happening and pull a gun. My first two shots were to their bodies, the next two to their heads as they slumped forward. The silencer reduced the noise of the shots to *phut*, *phut*, *phut*, *phut*, and no residents nearby would even know they'd been fired. Gold reached in and stubbed out the tell-tale cigarette that had dropped from one of the dead men's hands and closed the rear door.

'Next?' she asked.

'I'll check the flat and then I'll get rid of them.' I checked the front of the van; the keys were in the ignition.

I used my duplicate set of keys to get into the house and then into Janie's flat; 310666 still worked and the alarm events list showed nobody had come in since my last visit, so no need to check the rooms. I reset it and left. Gold was standing in the small front garden, shielded from view by a large hedge.

'Nobody's been in,' I told her.

'That's a good sign. What now?'

'I'll take the van and tidy things up. Been a long day – see what you can find out about the West London Cleaning Company in the morning, give me ring at home if anything shows up. I ought to go and see Marcia and Janie tomorrow, catch up on things and pick Marcia's brain on Randall's close friends – might get a name or two for the Essex driver. I'll give you a call.'

'Okay.' And she was gone, hardly noticeable in the dark as she made her way back to the Lexus. I got into the van and adjusted the seat – one of those stiffs in the back must have short legs – and then made a call on my mobile. It took a few rings before it was answered.

'Yeah?' said a tired voice.

'Ben Nevis, I have a job for you.'

'Mr Nevis, what are you doing getting us out of bed at this time of the night? Long time no see.'

'Yes, things have been a bit quiet on the personal removal part of the business lately, but I have urgent need of your services.'

'At this time of night? It's a bit late, even for you, Mr Nevis. Just one?'

'Two.'

'When?'

'Now.'

'Are you kidding?'

'No, I need to clear a motor before I get rid of it.'

'Hang on.' The voice said something away from the phone to another person. They had a muffled conversation, and he came back to me. 'How far away are you?'

'Thirty minutes.'

'Okay, we'll see you there.'

'Good man.'

'And Mr Nevis...'

'Yes, I know – cash.'

'Yes, five hundred each – and we haven't gone cashless payments just yet.'

Click.

****

The 'twins' had been good to me over the years. Both were now in their eighties and I still don't know their names – don't need to; all I know is they were introduced to me many years ago by a nasty piece of work as '*the best magicians in England*'. And they were, a '*magician*' in gangland parlance being somebody who makes things disappear; in the twins' case it was bodies. One thing a hitman needs is a magician; no dead body means no evidence, and no evidence means no arrest. Simple. I'd used their services eight times in the past without any problems; their heyday was when they were young, in the bad old days just after the Krays and Richardsons were sent down and a new breed of wannabes had fought for pieces of the London drugs turf. They'd laughed as they told me how '*business was brisk in those days*'. I guessed jobs were few and far between these days, because there's always a building site somewhere laying a thick concrete foundation that could take a body or two; and seeing that most of the big development sites in London are backed by mob money, it isn't a problem.

It took me a little over the thirty minutes to get to the twins' place of business, South London Crematorium. I flashed my headlights at the double iron gates and they swung slowly open, letting me through, and closed behind me. I drove along the drive, past the front entrance and round to the back delivery doors. The twins were waiting with two body bags and a trolley. Conversation wasn't needed, a couple of grunts that translated into, 'Hello, how jolly nice to see you Ben, are you keeping well?' – or maybe not. The money from my ankle wallet changed hands first; nice to see they still trusted me and didn't bother to count it.

I opened the van doors and working together we pulled out the two goons and laid them on the body bags. The twins stripped off any jewellery, rings, gold bracelets and neck chains; any finger that wouldn't release a ring was snipped beside the ring with a pair of industrial secateurs and the ring prised off. The twins probably made as much again as their fee with the little pile of goodies from these two stiffs. Pockets were checked for cash, and anything that could identify who the bodies were was left with them, which were then zipped into their body bags before being lifted onto the trolley and wheeled inside through the double doors. They stopped there and I took my cue to leave.

The doors closed as I got back into the van and made my way back round to the gates, which swung open as I approached and closed behind me when I'd left. I stopped a couple of hundred metres up the road, got out and looked back. The whisp of smoke from the crematorium chimney turned slowly into a small plume; the twins were working their magic. There wouldn't be much smoke, as the filters used by crematoriums these days to stay within the clean air laws strip out all the harmful bits. Job done.

I made my way back home and left the van in Gold's parking spot, before going up to my apartment, taking a shower and saying goodnight to the world.

CHAPTER 12

In the morning my stomach reminded me I hadn't eaten for some time. I looked in the kitchen cupboard at my usual bran flakes, raisins and walnuts and wasn't impressed, so I took a stroll out to the local greasy spoon and had a full English with a giant mug of tea. Mistake. Why do you always regret the loss of willpower? I regretted the full English as I trudged back to the apartment feeling bloated. I took a half hour session on my multi-gym and felt a bit better physically, but still my lack of willpower was annoying me. I needed to get stronger in that department. Gold's the same with chocolate; tells me she's never going to eat another bar and the next week her dashboard is a veritable hoard of Mars bars, Snickers and Milky Way wrappers.

I had work to do, so a quick shower and some fresh clothes and I felt better. I took the stairs down to the apartment foyer and gave the security guard the '*25% off your next full English*' voucher the greasy spoon had given me when I'd paid; looking at the guard's girth, I reckoned he was a regular. We exchanged a few pleasantries and I crossed to the door leading to the stairs down to the garage, with the guard's '*Have a nice day, Mr Hadlow*' getting a smile, and a '*You too*' from me.

The West London Cleaning Company van was still there, and I wondered if the Bogdans had missed it yet; they must have. I drove it to Deptford, nice and easy; stopping for people waiting at crossings, not pushing through amber lights. The last thing I wanted was a police stop and trying to explain the bloodstains in the back. I pulled into the yard of 'Deptford Scrap, Ferrous and Non Ferrous Metal Bought'. It was busy; two metallic cranes were lifting from piles of scrap and dumping it into a crusher, a line of written-off car crash vehicles stripped of anything saleable waiting for the same treatment. The crusher's jaws would render them into a five-foot square metal cube. I pulled up in front of a portacabin, gave a tap on the door and went inside.

'Ben Nevis, haven't seen you for ages.'

Annie Greggs was a chain-smoking Cockney, the epitome of mutton dressed as lamb. Pushing seventy-five, she had a blonde wig, make-up she must put on with a trowel, duck lips, Botox cheeks, breast implants to shame Dolly Parton, and wore miniskirts, fishnet stockings and high heel boots. She'd inherited the yard from her father who somehow ended up in his own crusher. She'd always maintained he'd slipped on the edge when a gear got stuck and was releasing it; others say he welshed on a debt to somebody he shouldn't have and paid the price. I don't know the truth. But I do know that

Annie is good at what she does; she doesn't suffer fools and has been known to lay out a heavy docker who ridiculed her appearance with one right-hander.

She was stood behind the counter looking out of the window to the yard. 'You got yourself a proper job at last have you, Ben – cleaning?'

I ignored that remark. 'How are you, Annie? You look busy.'

'Always busy, Ben. Great demand for steel these days, can't complain. What brings you here?'

'Well, my new job as a cleaner didn't work out – can't sell the van because of the sign writing, so I want it crushed.'

She smiled at me, not believing a word I'd said. 'Of course you do – and you've misplaced the registration documents too, haven't you Ben?'

'You know me so well, Annie.'

'Too well, Ben, too well. Urgent, is it?'

'Yes.'

'Five hundred notes urgent?'

Seems five hundred pounds is the going rate for everything. I'd stopped at an ATM on the way and refilled my ankle wallet. I knelt and pulled out eleven fifties and passed them over.

'You're a star, Annie. Take your latest toyboy for a decent meal.'

She laughed. 'You know me so well, Ben.'

'Too well, Annie, too well.'

'Come on then, let's get it done. Cash is king.'

She led the way outside and crossed to one of the magnetic cranes and shouted up to the driver and pointed to the van. He nodded, dropped his load of scrap back on the heap and swung the jib round over the van, switched on the magnet and dropped it onto the roof with bang. The van was lifted up, over the other cars and held waiting, swinging slowly above the crusher as the last heap of metal slid out in box form onto the conveyor belt from the jaws as they opened like a hungry shark, and the hydraulic shaft pushed it out. The magnet was turned off and West London Cleaning Company's van fell into the jaws. The power of them closing on and squashing the van was quite frightening; if Annie's dad had been alive inside the pit as they closed, he probably died of fright before they ate him. The van came out as a box in a matter of minutes; it was dripping oil and petrol as the magnetic crane lifted it into its place onto a pile of similar squashed metal boxes.

Annie turned to me. 'Well, at least there wasn't anybody in the back of it.'

'How can you tell?'

'Blood is a different colour to oil.' She laughed and added quickly. 'So I'm told.'

I pecked her cheek. 'Thanks for that.'

'Anytime, Ben. Don't be a stranger – pop in and say hello from time to time.'

'I'll try.'

'That's what all the nice boys say, but they never do.'

We laughed together and I gave a wave and a thumbs-up to the crane driver and walked from the yard. Job done.

CHAPTER 13

Clancy rung; he wanted a meet, but wouldn't say why. I arranged to see him at Charing Cross in an hour, giving me time to check in with Gold. I gave her a call. She hadn't dug anything up on the West London Cleaning Company; in fact she said she sensed a wall of silence coming up every time she mentioned it to her street contacts.

Clancy wasn't a happy bunny. I got two cups of British Rail dishwater when he arrived and sat back, prepared for a bollocking.

'My friends in Romania are not very happy with you.'

'I rescued a kidnap victim, a British National, held by a Romanian drugs family.'

'There are diplomatic channels open to use for that.'

'Really, like the Diplomatic channels that are open for Nazanin Zaghari-Ratcliffe?'

'That's above my pay grade, Nevis – you wreaking havoc and killing Romanian nationals in Romania isn't.'

'Don't know what you mean.'

Clancy let out a long sigh; he was fed up with me. I'd better tread a bit more lightly.

'I have CCTV footage sent from Romania of you with Janie Johnson on an underground station – a station where two stabbings took place. I have various still photos they have cut from various retail CCTV cameras of you in amongst a crowd running from that station. I have CCTV footage of four men being shot at the Debrecen border post by somebody looking suspiciously like you and a female accomplice, together with Janie Johnson in a hired car. The car was rented at Debrecen airport and returned a short time later, just before a private charter flight left there for Stansted. I seem to recall meeting you, your partner and Janie off a private charter flight at Stansted. I've checked, and it came in from Debrecen. So cut the bullshit and let's figure out what we are going to do to avoid an international incident and the Home Secretary going up the wall.'

I didn't say a word, sometimes silence is the best policy. Clancy took a gulp of BR dishwater, grimaced and carried on. 'Lucky for you, Nevis, I have regular dealings with my opposite number in Romania. We have been working on eliminating the Bogdan family both there and here – and by eliminating I mean by legal methods through the courts. So far you have eliminated three of the five brothers by illegal methods, Alexandru here and two over there. That leaves, according to my sources, two brothers, Danut and Stefan, who they believe are in the UK. I told you before that we are monitoring the family, the reason being that a joint strike would be made in Romania and here when we are ready, with enough evidence to put the family away for many years. They were going about their illegal business quite unaware of our surveillance, until you started a war with them.'

'Hang on, they started it – they kidnapped Janie. I was just getting her back for my client, Marcia Johnson.' I was sounding like a schoolboy in the head's study, '*He started it, sir, not me.*'

'Doesn't matter who started it, Nevis, it's got the Bogdan family worried and running around like blue-arsed flies – and, I may also add, put Marcia Johnson well into their firing line. The last thing we want is for the Bogdans to close their drug supply business now – we know where they operate from and how they distribute. Another few weeks and we will have enough evidence to bring them down and put them away. So back off – you've got Janie back, so back off.'

My mind was racing; if Clancy and his Romanian partners were going to bring the Bogdans down, then that left an awful lot of money in an Isle of Man account that they wouldn't be able to do anything about it whilst sitting in their cells. Be a nice bonus to the job if I could whip in and get my hands on it.

'Ever heard of the West London Cleaning Company?' I thought I'd ask; Clancy might know where that fitted in. I didn't expect the result I got; he nearly choked on his dishwater and I had to thump his back to clear his windpipe.

'Don't even go there, Nevis – strictly off the grid, out of bounds.'

'I've already been there.'

'Oh Jesus!' His face sank with despair, 'What, when?'

'Last night, two goons were sitting in a West London Cleaning Company van outside Janie's flat waiting for her to return – probably going to grab her again. There was a business flyer from that company on her table the first time I went there after she'd been taken.'

'And you did what last night?'

'They're gone.'

'Gone? Gone where?'

'Just gone, disappeared.'

Clancy knew what I was saying. 'Where's the van?'

'Gone, disappeared.'

He sat back in his chair and pondered things for quite a while before speaking again. 'West London Cleaners is a Bogdan cover company. Being a cleaner and dry cleaner they can order quantities of chemicals without any problem – chemicals they use in the production of crystal meth, the most addictive drug on the market, and a killer. They get the basic cocaine and upgrade it in their factory, which masquerades as a fabric cleaning plant. We have it under surveillance, and as I said, in a couple of weeks, when the Romanians are ready, we will raid it and close the Bogdans down once and for all.'

'And the van?'

'They use – or should I say used – it to deliver the finished product in single tabs to their street wholesalers, who sell on to the postcode gangs. All very professional.'

'So they'll miss the van straight away, won't they?' That worried me.

'Of course they will, and the two men that were with it. This throws up a bigger problem – if they suspect OC have taken it and have their men in custody, they'll get jittery and might close down and run.' He stood up. 'Go home, Nevis, and stay there – no more heroics. I need to talk to some people and then I'll get back to you.' He turned to go. 'And I hope you've a black tie for tomorrow.'

'Tomorrow?'

'Harry Cohen's funeral, eleven a.m. Golder's Green Cemetery. Be interesting to see who turns up.'

And he left in a hurry, looking worried.

CHAPTER 14

The cemetery was big enough for Gold and I to stay a good hundred metres away from the Cohen funeral party gathered around the grave for the ceremony. Gold had brought a camera with a telescopic lens with her and took lots of pictures of the mourners. It was a good crowd. We had positioned ourselves beside a large old oak tree, giving us a good amount of cover. I noticed Clancy representing the police, a few of Harry's business friends and some people obviously from his talent roster. They were easy to pick out as they kept turning towards the few media photographers twenty metres away, hoping for a picture of themselves in the tabloids or entertainment media the next day. No publicity is bad publicity, even if it is at your agent's graveside. Assholes.

Marcia and Janie were there in sombre garb, and I noticed four pretty obvious plainclothes officers hanging nearby. Harry's widow was easy to pick out by her position nearest to the priest, or rabbi – not sure what to call him at a Jewish funeral. The widow had a young man in his thirties beside her, whom I took to be Harry's son, and a lady of about the same age who must be his daughter. He'd mentioned them once but hadn't gone into any detail.

I wondered if his wife had known about his 'illegal' career? How had Clancy explained Harry being shot to the family?

Gold jarred my elbow. 'Bandits three o'clock.'

I looked and saw two goons – pretty obvious by their appearance: flowing overcoats, hands in pockets – a good distance away. I stepped back behind the oak just in case they were looking for me. A picture of me may well have made its way to the Bogdans, or what was left of them, via friends in the Romanian police. Gold snapped them before stepping back with me.

'You think they are checking on Janie?' she asked.

I nodded. 'Could well be – mind you, to try and take her again would be daft.'

'Still a million quid in play in an account they think Marcia has access to.'

'True.'

Harry's coffin was lowered into the grave, the wife's wreath was lowered onto it and the party left, shaking hands with the priest or rabbi as they made their way to the car park. The goons left too, hurrying away before the funeral party

****

Back at my office Gold loaded the camera SIM card into her laptop as I made a coffee to have with beef and horseradish rolls I'd bought from the deli opposite. I sat back and watched as she pulled up the pictures one by one. Was Randall's mysterious driver/accomplice amongst the mourners? Perhaps the last two Bogdan brothers were at the graveside? I wouldn't know what they looked like, but they might well have been there, and the two goons might just have been their protection. I recognised a couple of the Z-list celebrities; couldn't name them, but their duck lips and Botox faces seemed familiar. I chastised myself for watching too much crap telly.

'Whoa…'

'What?'

'Go back to the last one.' I leant nearer to the screen.

Gold clicked back to the last picture, the young man beside Harry's wife.

'Harry's son, Avram,' Gold told me.

I'd had a flashback when the face hit the screen: a flashback to Izvor underground station and the goons running in from the road as I knelt by the wall pretending to tie a shoelace. This face was one of them, I was sure.

'He was one of Bogdan's men that ran into Izvor station. I'm positive.'

'Positive?'

'Yes.'

'Are you saying Harry Cohen's son works for Bogdan?'

'That man was at Izvor, one hundred percent.'

My mobile buzzed. It was Clancy; he wasn't happy. There's a surprise.

'You've upset the apple cart taking that van – there's increased activity around West London Cleaners' premises. Looks like they're moving stuff out, so we are going in with AROs at four o'clock.'

'Am I invited?'

'Why not? Your actions are probably responsible for it.'

'Where is it?'

'Clapham Industrial Estate, know it?'

'I'm a private detective, not an estate agent.'

'Yes, well, you rank equal in my estimation.' Clancy can be hurtful.

I humoured him. 'Ha ha. Where is it?'

'Union Road, Clapham – meet me by the gate at 3.45 and stay out of sight. If they know your face and see you, they'll realise something's definitely up and run a mile.'

I told Gold what was happening. We continued through the pictures but none of the rest struck a chord. Something was bothering me.

‘So if Harry Cohen’s son is working for the Bogdans, *they* wouldn’t kill Harry, would they?’

‘If they did, the question is why?’

‘But they’ve no reason to – if Harry knew where the missing money was he’d tell them, he’d want to keep on their good side for future business. He’d have no reason not to tell them, and they’d have no reason to kill him – no reason at all.’

Gold shut the laptop. ‘Which leaves the question, who killed Harry?’

‘And why?’

‘Well, two reasons to kill him. One, the killer wanted information out of Harry that he wouldn’t or couldn’t give them – or two, he knew who the Randall accomplice was who has the money and was threatening to tell the Bogdans, so the accomplice killed him.’

‘It’s a bit of a jigsaw, isn’t it.’

‘Yes, and the final piece is still missing.’

CHAPTER 15

Outside the Clapham Industrial Estate I pulled up behind two ARVs full of AROs in full attack gear, from their helmets to their boots. Behind them, two minibuses of uniformed officers and a couple of plain cars with OCOs waited silently. Clancy wandered over.

'The Bogdans' unit is a single ground floor warehouse, fifty metres by thirty. The windows have strong grilles welded over them and are blacked out. The door is steel with no outside handle – it's a typical drug factory. I've got twenty AROs going in after they blow the door in. There's a back door, all steel again, so I've armed plainclothes round there in case some make a run for it that way.'

'What if there's a tunnel?' I remembered the one at the club in Bucharest.

'A tunnel? This is Clapham, Nevis, not Colditz. Here, take this so you can follow what's happening.' He passed me a radio. 'And stay here until we've got the place locked down and safe. Then you can come and take a look, see if you recognise anybody.' He walked off.

Gold and I watched as the AROs left their vehicles and moved quickly in single file, their MP5SFA3 semi-automatic carbines clutched to their chests, fingers on trigger. The uniforms followed with the plain clothes OCOs. The line disappeared quickly into the industrial estate. We could hear the instructions through the radio.

'Line against the sidewalls. When the door goes in, we go in. Be alert, these bastards are probably armed.' There was a short pause, then, *'All ready to go, sir.'*

Clancy gave the order. 'In your own time, sergeant.'

There was a silence and then the crack of an explosive charge going off and lots of shouting. *'Armed police,' 'Lay down, armed police', 'Stay where you are, armed police', 'Armed police'...* Then silence.

Clancy's voice. 'What's happening sergeant?'

'Place is empty, sir.'

'Can't be, surveillance saw eighteen people go in this morning and nobody's left.'

'It's empty, sir.'

Gold and I exchanged knowing glances as I started the car and swung it round in the road, the tyres screeching a protest. I was going to follow the streets that ran along outside the boundary of the estate until we found what we knew would be there. One of the roads was a one way coming towards me; Clancy could pay my fine if a camera caught me. I hurtled down it with the oncoming traffic braking to a halt either side; I could do with a magnetic blue light to whack on the roof, must get one. All the time Gold and I had our eyes firmly fixed on the road ahead; we both knew what we were looking for, and on the fourth turn at a junction we saw it. A hundred metres ahead the road surface was disgorging people from an open manhole; a few pedestrians not quite believing what they were seeing stood looking in amazement. I noticed Gold had her gun out. Two men were stood beside the manhole helping others out. They turned and saw us; when they realised we were not going to stop, they took out guns and started firing at us. They had let go of the person they were hauling out of the manhole who dropped back into the hole, banging his head like a bagatelle ball in play on the rim as he fell. Ouch! I felt that! But I had to smile.

I swerved the car as they loosed off more shots at us and the tyres screamed their pain as I stood on the brakes to bring it to a halt sideways on towards the shooters. Gold was out of the passenger door, and shielded by the car pumped bullets towards our targets; from twenty metres she doesn't miss. One fell to the ground, blood soaking through his T-shirt from four holes around his heart and one in his neck; his gun fell from his hand and skated away on the tarmac. The other turned to run, but out in the open he had no chance. My first shot took his left leg from under him, and my second entered the back of his head as he fell. We left the car and approached the open manhole slowly from either side, expecting a head and a gun to appear, but it didn't. The nearest shooter that Gold had taken out was lying on his front. I turned him over with my boot. Avram Cohen's dead eyes were open but seeing nothing. The second man I didn't know, but he wasn't an Asian worker, so I hoped he was a Bogdan.

I heard the sound of metal sliding on the tarmac and saw Gold kicking the manhole cover back in position, blocking the escape route. I hadn't taken much notice of the radio and had left it in the car, but now I could hear Clancy screaming down it from twenty metres away. I walked to the car and picked it up from the floor.

'Nevis here.'

'*Where are you, what's happening? We heard shots, what's going on?*'

'Somewhere in the warehouse you'll find a trapdoor leading to an escape tunnel.'

'Yes, we found that.'

'I'm at the other end, it comes out on one of the boundary roads – just follow the perimeter of the industrial estate and you'll find us. There's a load of workers in the tunnel, they may retrace their steps back to the warehouse so keep officers there. We've blocked off this end – bring a wagon and some officers here and we'll open it up. Oh, and get a doctor.'

'Is somebody injured?'

'No, dead. You know the rules, a doctor must certify the person dead before you can remove the body – or in this case, bodies.'

'Oh Christ, Nevis, how many?'

'Two, one? I don't know. The other is Harry Cohen's son.'

There was a pause. *'Harry Cohen's son?'*

'Yes, Harry Cohen's son. I'll explain when you get here.'

****

Clancy took a deep breath, 'What a bloody game, eh?'

An hour later he was standing beside my car with me and Gold. The street had been cordoned off at either end to keep the media away, although with telescopic lenses it wouldn't do. The last of the Korean drug workers were being helped out of the manhole and shepherded into a Social Services coach to be taken to an immigrant detention centre.

Gold felt sorry for them. 'Poor bastards, I bet they came here thinking the sun was about to shine on their lives.'

The OIC joined us with a sheaf of papers in his hand. 'The translator says they say they came in the back of lorries from Romania.'

Clancy nodded. 'Makes sense, another of the Bogdan's income streams.'

The IOC continued. 'We have two Romanians in custody who seem to be part of the gang management of the place. They've identified one of the dead as Stefan Bogdan and can't name the other, but say he's English.'

Clancy nodded. 'Yes, we know who he is.' He turned to me. 'And then there was one, eh? If Stefan is dead, that leaves Danut.'

I smiled. 'He's going to be a bit pissed off by now, isn't he? All his brothers dead – the family back home aren't going to like that.'

Clancy checked his watch. 'The rest of the family should all be in custody by now – Romanian police were doing a simultaneous raid on The Amsterdam Club at the same time as we went in here. From what I can gather there's only the father that holds any sway other than the brothers, so I should think the dealers they supply will be off as soon as news of the raids breaks. They certainly won't be buying from the Bogdans in future.'

Two police motorcyclists pulled up and two dog handlers jumped off the pillions; the IOC gave them a nod and spoke into his radio. All three waited by the manhole with two AROs who had their rifles aimed at it. The IOC turned and explained. ‘They’re letting the dogs into the tunnel at the other end – anybody hiding down there now will get a shock.’

The tunnel was clear, and the dogs emerged and collected their reward treats from the handlers.

‘Shame that.’ I looked at Clancy. ‘I was quite looking forward to seeing Danut Bogdan coming out with a dog hanging on each leg.’

Clancy looked at me and shook his head unbelievably. ‘Nevis, I think you should go get counselling.’

Funny that, ‘cause, as you know I sometimes think that too. I turned to Gold for support, but she was nodding in agreement with Clancy.

CHAPTER 16

Danut Bogdan was first out of the tunnel. The CCTV camera had picked up the AROs coming towards the warehouse; the camera had been fitted on a vacant building opposite and covered the warehouse approach. It was wireless, so nobody knew the monitor screen was in the warehouse. Stephan had thought of that; Stephan's good like that, Stephan sorted things out. Stephan had had the escape tunnel built; it was easy, it dropped from the warehouse floor into a major electricity mains cable access tunnel built to service the industrial estate many years ago and forgotten as the place expanded. It was six-foot high and narrow, with various cables hooked along the walls. It was wide enough to get along sideways to the steel stairs at the end that led up to the manhole. Stephan had given Danut a torch, and he and Avram had followed him into the tunnel with the rest of the workers scrambling in behind them. At the end it took a few hits with a sledgehammer kept there for just that reason to shift the cover and push it aside. The street was empty as Danut hauled himself out and gave Stephan a helping hand.

'Go and fetch the minibus,' Stephan told Danut as he leant to help Avram out. 'Bring it here and we'll get the workers into it.'

Danut ran towards the end of the road; he'd parked the minibus two streets away after dropping the workers off at the warehouse that morning. As he reached the end of the road he heard gunshots behind him, and turning round looked back to where a car had slewed sideways and stopped fifty metres away from the other side of the manhole; two people were firing at Stephan and Avram who were firing back. Avram fell down; Danut reached into his jacket for his gun and started back. Stephan fell; he was still, and neither Stephan nor Avram were moving. Danut thought quickly. The two people with the guns were good; no warning had been shouted, no '*armed police, drop your weapons*', nothing; so the two in the car were not AROs, not police; whoever they were they would be more than a match for him. He turned and walked quickly away from the scene, his brain scrambled. He needed to get to safety and work things out.

Danut took a train from Clapham Junction to Euston and then the underground to Aldgate East and walked the rest of the way down Commercial Road to the Bucharest Club. It was shut, of course, as it was still a crime scene with police tape across the front. Forensics had been in and finished their work and the place was empty. The local council had quickly revoked the music licence, so to all intents and purposes the club was dead. The landlords had taken back the lease by court order and now it stood empty, waiting for the police to release it to the landlords.

Danut went up the side alleyway and let himself in by the side door. He sat down in Alexandru's old office; the electricity was still on, and a bare bulb hung from the ceiling. The stain from his brother's spilt blood showed on the desk and floor, highlighted by the forensic officer's luminol spray. His mind had settled, but his anger had risen. The reports from Romania on the rescue of the hostage had mentioned two people, a male and female; the two at the manhole could be them, he had been too far away to notice if one was female. They had to be the same pair, but who were they? Had they killed Harry Cohen too? And now Harry's son? The whole organisation was being brought down.

His mobile rang; it was Romania. He took the call and listened to more bad news. The club in Bucharest had been raided; his father and most of the other gang members were arrested and the cocaine bricks seized. The Bogdans were finished; he was the only family member left. If Stephan was wounded but alive, he'd surely go to prison for life. No, Danut was the one free survivor, and Danut was going to avenge his family. He needed to find out who the pair of mercenaries were, and who hired them. He broke the crime scene seal on Alexandru's desk drawers and rummaged through. He found what he was looking for, a file with James Randall's name on it; inside the information was in Romanian. He read it; it told him all that he wanted to know.

CHAPTER 17

'I'm so very grateful, Mr Nevis, I really am. It's been an awful time, and to think Harry Cohen was involved all along and must have known where Janie was all the time.'

Marcia Johnson was sitting in her lounge beside Janie and holding her daughter's hand tightly. Clancy had deemed it was okay for them to return home now, although a police presence was being kept at the house for the time being until Danut Bogdan was found. 'No wonder he wouldn't let me call the police.'

'I told you he was no good ages ago, mother, but you wouldn't listen.'

'Well, I knew he wasn't a great agent, dear, but I'd been with him for so long, he was like family. Had I known he was dealing drugs and working with your late father I would have walked away, of course I would. I feel so sorry for his wife, losing a husband and a son like that.'

'Bad apples the pair of them,' I said. 'Think of all the pain and misery their drugs brought to people over the years.'

Gold and I had driven out to Marcia's house to make sure they were both okay, and happy for me to close my involvement with them. Oh, and to give Marcia my bill. It was a heavy one, what with the charter flight and hotel bills – totalled a hundred and twenty thousand, but she didn't baulk at it. By the time I'd paid the charter and reimbursed Gold for her flights and our hotel and vehicles in Romania, we'd be left with fifty thousand each. That's okay, but I think Marcia got a bargain for saving her daughter's life. Nothing more I could do now: hostage back home, the Bogdans out of the picture – except for Danut, but he wasn't in the tunnel so Clancy thought he'd be in Romania trying to rescue whatever he could of the family business. Criminals like the Bogdans use fake passports by the bucketload, so he might be in the UK, but not likely. And then there was the missing money which brought the whole thing about. It was sitting in a bank in the Isle of Man and untouchable except by Randall's partner, whoever that was. Not my problem. My job was done. I rose to leave.

'Well, it's been a pleasure to be of help, Mrs Johnson. I'll be watching Janie's career with interest.'

Janie laughed. 'You'll get tickets for the West End, Mr Nevis, be assured of that – best seats in the house.' She stood and gave me an embarrassing peck on the cheek. 'By the way, you never did tell me, how did you become a hitman?'

I smiled and gave a little shrug. ‘Pure luck, I was first in line at the Job Centre that day.’

CHAPTER 18

Gold dropped me off at the office. I offered to take her out for a celebratory meal, but she had a wealthy client eager to part with some of his wealth for her attention. I had a bundle of mail waiting on the floor where it had been poked through the letterbox; mostly bills, no doubt, but you never know – could be a damsel in distress seeking my services amongst them. Never has been in the past, but hope springs eternal.

I picked them up and settled down to go through them when the door opened and Danut Bogdan came in, pointing a gun straight at my head. My Beretta was in the righthand desk drawer, and if I made a move for it I'd be dead. I stayed silent. He walked to the front of my desk, took an iPhone from his jacket pocket, clicked on a video and held it towards me so I could see the screen.

'You.'

The video was the CCTV footage taken at the Hungarian-Romanian border; it showed Gold pulling up in the Range Rover and the carnage as she and I shot the goons and bumped over one as we left.

'You.'

'No, not me.'

'Yes, you, Mr Nevis. You killed my brothers, and now I will kill you.'

I played for time. 'Doesn't even look like me. I've got a limp, that's not me.'

He laughed. 'You haven't got a limp. I am not stupid, Mr Nevis. Alexandru kept a file on Randall and Cohen. I watched you at Randall's wife's house an hour ago. No limp. How would you like to die, Mr Nevis? I think slowly would be good – a bullet in each leg, and then each arm, and then finally the head.'

'Why waste four bullets? One to the head will do.' I was thinking that I would push up the desk from my side quickly towards him. If I was quick enough, any bullets he fired might lodge in it.

'You don't deserve to die quickly. You have five seconds to pray.'

Pray? Me? If there is a God, he gave up on me long ago.

'Five… four…' I tensed my arms ready to move. 'Three… two...'

'ONE.' It wasn't Danut's voice. He turned quickly to see Gold standing in the doorway, her gun held two-handed and pointing his way. A small puff of smoke left the end of the silencer long after the bullet left a jagged exit wound in Danut Bogdan's head. He fell sideways onto the desk, blood seeping onto my mail.

I felt I should embrace her and thank her for saving my life, but me and Gold, we don't do embracing.

'I thought you had business to see to?'

'It can wait. I changed my mind about the meal – not often you buy.'

I smiled. Gold has a way of trivialising things; things like a dead body across my desk.

'He followed us from Marcia's,' I explained.

'You sure there aren't any more Bogdan brothers likely to pop out of the woodwork?'

'No, Clancy said there were five so he's the last – two at the border post and three here.' I showed her the video on Danut's phone. 'I need Clancy to get his mates in Romania to destroy that.' I took the SIM card out and flushed it down the toilet. 'Right, we'd better get rid of this body.'

I gave the twins a call.

'You're like the buses, Nevis – none for ages and three come at once. You'll want wholesale rates next.' He laughed. 'How many this time?'

'Just one.'

'Ready now?'

'Yes.'

'Give us an hour, see you there – and Nevis...'

'I know, cash only.'

'That's right,'
Click.

CHAPTER 19

It was past three o'clock in the morning when we got back from the crematorium. We'd taken my car with Danut wrapped in plastic bin bags in the boot. Too late for that meal; I did offer to take Gold for a cheeseburger on Battersea Bridge, but the offer was declined. She said she'd come round to the office in the afternoon and give me a hand breaking up the desk and taking it to the tip. I could paint it over, but you never know; evidence is what law enforcement lives on, and I never leave any.

I slept well; my mind was free, no plans buzzing round it of how to get Janie back, or what was happening with Harry Cohen – all done and dusted, case closed, job done. If Clancy wanted to chase the missing money, he was welcome to. Not my problem.

Gold turned up at the office after lunch and the desk came apart pretty easily. After throwing it into the skip at the local council tip she persuaded me to detour on the way back to Ikea and buy a new flat pack desk, which we managed to put together in half an hour. I arranged my leather blotter, the phone and the laptop on it. All very professional looking. We sat with a coffee as Gold checked her mobile trying to find an expensive restaurant to book. She was determined to get that meal out of me.

My laptop beeped, incoming mail. I checked it; an email from Marcia thanking me once more and saying my fee had been sent through. I checked my bank account; it had, all one hundred and twenty thousand was sitting in my account.

'Marcia's paid,' I told Gold as I pulled up the '*Pay Somebody or a Business'* page on my bank site and put the figure fifty thousand in. 'What's your account? I'll transfer your share.'

'I'll do it.' She came round the desk and tapped in her account number. 'Not that I don't trust you with my account number Ben, but, I don't trust you with my account number Ben.'

I had to smile. I was about to press *pay* when Gold stayed my hand. 'Now that *is* interesting.'

'What is?'

'The account Marcia Johnson sent the money from is held at an Isle of Man Bank.'

THE END

Thank you for buying this book. If you enjoyed it please leave a review or rating on Amazon as that would mean an awful lot to me. Thank you.

To see more books in this series and others and get updates on new releases check my website:

www.barry-faulkner.com

Whilst there you may also like to sign up to my newsletter and receive advance notice of new books, freebies and other interesting posts. You can unsubscribe at any time and it's all FREE!!

Printed in Great Britain
by Amazon

61382474R00092